WHO HAD BLUDGEONED
THE BODY AT FRAZER'S MILLS?

THE CARRINGTONS—Lydia, the stunning spinster, and Lawrence, her dapper brother. Their father had discouraged their careers and dissuaded them from marrying, but was that reason to kill him?

MRS. TURNBULL—She had come to the exclusive Edgewood Rest Home to recover from her grief. Were her white minks and dazzling emeralds designed for mourning?

MR. MOTLEY—Had love of leisure brought him to the tiny village or did the handsome playboy have interests closer to his heart?

ROSE JENNER—Her dissolute father and her fame as a child chess prodigy gave her a curious past. Was there something so sinister she'd kill to keep it secret?

GARY YATES—If he'd come to town simply seeking shelter for the night, why was he lying about his identity and his friends?

Murder Ink.® Mysteries

1 DEATH IN THE MORNING, Sheila Radley
3 THE BRANDENBURG HOTEL,
Pauline Glen Winslow
5 McGARR AND THE SIENESE CONSPIRACY,
Bartholomew Gill
7 THE RED HOUSE MYSTERY, A. A. Milne
9 THE MINUTEMAN MURDERS, Jane Langton
11 MY FOE OUTSTRETCH'D BENEATH THE TREE,
V. C. Clinton-Baddeley
13 GUILT EDGED, W. J. Burley
15 COPPER GOLD, Pauline Glen Winslow
17 MANY DEADLY RETURNS, *Patricia Moyes*
19 McGARR AT THE DUBLIN HORSE SHOW,
Bartholomew Gill
21 DEATH AND LETTERS, Elizabeth Daly
23 ONLY A MATTER OF TIME,
V. C. Clinton-Baddeley
25 WYCLIFFE AND THE PEA-GREEN BOAT,
W. J. Burley
27 ANY SHAPE OR FORM, Elizabeth Daly
29 COFFIN SCARCELY USED, Colin Watson
31 THE CHIEF INSPECTOR'S DAUGHTER,
Sheila Radley
33 PREMEDICATED MURDER, Douglas Clark
35 NO CASE FOR THE POLICE, V. C. Clinton-Baddeley
37 JUST WHAT THE DOCTOR ORDERED,
Colin Watson
39 DANGEROUS DAVIES, Leslie Thomas
41 THE GIMMEL FLASK, Douglas Clark
43 SERVICE OF ALL THE DEAD, Colin Dexter
45 DEATH'S BRIGHT DART, V. C. Clinton-Baddeley
47 GOLDEN RAIN, Douglas Clark
49 THE MAN WITH A LOAD OF MISCHIEF,
Martha Grimes
51 DOWN AMONG THE DEAD MEN, Patricia Moyes
53 HOPJOY WAS HERE, Colin Watson
55 NIGHT WALK, Elizabeth Daly

Scene of the Crime® Mysteries

2 A MEDIUM FOR MURDER, Mignon Warner
4 DEATH OF A MYSTERY WRITER, Robert Barnard
6 DEATH AFTER BREAKFAST, Hugh Pentecost
8 THE POISONED CHOCOLATES CASE,
Anthony Berkeley
10 A SPRIG OF SEA LAVENDER, J.R.L. Anderson
12 WATSON'S CHOICE, Gladys Mitchell
14 SPENCE AND THE HOLIDAY MURDERS,
Michael Allen
16 THE TAROT MURDERS, Mignon Warner
18 DEATH ON THE HIGH C's, Robert Barnard
20 WINKING AT THE BRIM, Gladys Mitchell
22 TRIAL AND ERROR, Anthony Berkeley
24 RANDOM KILLER Hugh Pentecost
26 SPENCE AT THE BLUE BAZAAR, Michael Allen
28 GENTLY WITH THE INNOCENTS, Alan Hunter
30 THE JUDAS PAIR, Jonathan Gash
32 DEATH OF A LITERARY WIDOW, Robert Barnard
34 THE TWELVE DEATHS OF CHRISTMAS,
Marian Babson
36 GOLD BY GEMINI, Jonathan Gash
38 LANDED GENTLY, Alan Hunter
40 MURDER, MURDER, LITTLE STAR,
Marian Babson
42 DEATH IN A COLD CLIMATE, Robert Barnard
44 A CHILD'S GARDEN OF DEATH, Richard Forrest
46 GENTLY THROUGH THE WOODS, Alan Hunter
48 THE GRAIL TREE, Jonathan Gash
50 RULING PASSION, Reginald Hill
52 DEATH OF A PERFECT MOTHER, Robert Barnard
54 A COFFIN FROM THE PAST, Gwendoline Butler
56 AND ONE FOR THE DEAD, Pierre Audemars

A Murder Ink.® Mystery

NIGHT WALK

Elizabeth Daly

A DELL BOOK

Published by
DELL PUBLISHING CO., INC.
1 Dag Hammarskjold Plaza
New York, New York 10017

For information contact Dell Publishing Co., Inc.
Dell ® TM 681510, Dell Publishing Co., Inc.

ISBN: 0-440-15996-2

Reprinted by arrangement with the author.
Printed in the United States of America
First Dell printing—December 1982

DD

CONTENTS

1. *At Edgewood*   9
2. *At the Library*   15
3. *At the Wakefield Inn*   19
4. *At the Carringtons'*   30
5. *Psychological*   37
6. *The Facts*   52
7. *Descendants*   65
8. *Case Histories*   76
9. *Inside Stuff*   86
10. *Monsters*   96
11. *Criminology*   107
12. *Eliminations*   114
13. *Triumph of Vines*   126
14. *Clearance*   134
15. *The Trellis*   143
16. *Obsession*   155
17. *Evidence*   166
18. *Love Letter*   172
19. *Night Walk*   180

1. AT EDGEWOOD

It was not yet ten o'clock, but Miss Martine Studley, proprietor of Edgewood, came into the lounge and tactfully discouraged her four patients from beginning another rubber of bridge. August 26th, 1946, had been a close, warm day for the time of year, and it was a stuffy night. The patients looked bored with the game, all but old Mrs. Norbury; and if old Mrs. Norbury wasn't dog-tired, thought Miss Studley, she ought to be.

Miss Studley never described her guests as "patients," nor would she allow Edgewood to be referred to as a sanatorium or even a rest cure. It was simply a place where persons (very well-off persons) who had been sick or were overworked or merely needed a little country air could go and be sure of what attention they required. If they were really ill, or disabled, Miss Studley wouldn't take them. They were all sent to Edgewood by expensive doctors who were well aware that Miss Studley had filled a need.

Alcoholics or other addicts, mental cases and people likely to depress other people, were taboo. The doctors fully understood this, and it was only after long telephone conversations with Miss Studley that reservations at Edgewood were made.

Miss Studley was a graduate nurse, who had made such a huge success of private nursing (she had had two substantial legacies) that she was able to buy the fine old house at the edge of the woods and remodel it. She had an assistant, Miss Pepper, who gave massage. Edgewood, thus christened by its present owner, was ideally situated for her purpose—in the little village of Frazer's Mills, five miles from the big town of Westbury and the railroad, two and a half hours' journey by car from New York. It was open all the year round. It stood well back from the street, the last house of the village to the north, with large shady grounds and its own vegetable garden.

Miss Studley was a well-built, good-looking woman of forty with fresh color and a great deal of thick brown hair. She always wore her uniform and cap; they gave the guests confidence. She knew exactly how to treat people who were not quite well and wanted attention but no nagging and no rules. There were no rules at Edgewood except doctors' orders that came with the guests.

On this Thursday before Labor Day there were only four guests, two men and two women, and they were not very well assorted this time. There was old Mrs. Norbury, a repeater, from Long Island, who had a mild form of arthritis; a Mrs. Turnbull from Pittsburgh, recently widowed, in her forties, charted as "run-down"; a business man of sixty from New York named Haynes, who had a heart condition. Edgewood was just right for him—invigorating but not too high, a nice change from the city; and a youngish man from a Jersey suburb, named Motley, sent as an obstinate case of trigeminal neuralgia.

Fortunately they were all bridge players.

Miss Studley came into the lounge, watched them finish the rubber and tot up the score, and then asked them if they didn't think they might as well call it a day.

"Just as you like, of course," she said in her cheerful way. "Sit up all night if you like. But Mrs. Norbury is practically off the train, and Miss Pepper wants to give her massage. Anybody hungry? Miss Pepper will come right up with eggnog or iced cocoa if you are."

Nobody was hungry except old Mrs. Norbury, who had the digestion of an ostrich and meant to order an iced cocoa as soon as she went upstairs.

Mrs. Turnbull, a tall woman with a set, foolish smile, who played a wicked game of contract, got up and said she was all ready to go to bed and read. She said goodnight, and tottered up the stairs on high-heeled gilt slippers. Warm as the evening was, she wore a white fur wrap. When she was out of sight Mrs. Norbury cackled: "Early fall fashions for the country."

Miss Studley thought a little intramural gossip was good for the guests. She said: "I never saw anything like that emerald bracelet."

"Those pearls real, I wonder?" asked Mr. Motley. He was a rather handsome man of thirty, tanned and black-haired, with a cool, competent look about him. He had been in Washington during the war, and was now looking about, so he said, for a business opening.

"Real? Certainly," said Mrs. Norbury. "Her second-best string, no doubt."

"And ermine!" Miss Studley looked impressed.

"Ermine? My dear woman, that is a white mink dolman."

"Is it? What would it cost?"

"About thirty thousand, I suppose. Or more."

"Well, well," said Mr. Haynes. He was a tall gray-headed man with a gray moustache, well-turned out and very quiet. He seldom talked to anybody.

"Golf tomorrow, sir?" asked Motley, rising. "If so I'll go up and read in bed myself."

"Very glad to play. Too bad you haven't somebody in your own class."

"You'll both soon find partners at the Westbury Club," said Miss Studley. Edgewood guests usually did find partners at the club, through friends or their doctors; or Miss Studley arranged it through friends of her own. She had been born and brought up in Frazer's Mills, commonly known as The Mills, and knew everybody for miles around.

The guests went up the stairs that rose gracefully in a curve from the north end of the lobby. Miss Studley turned out all the lights, left the front door open until later, and went upstairs herself. She had no office on the ground floor; her theory being that Edgewood ought to look like a country-house and not like an institution. Her

11

office sitting room was on the top floor. No guest could possibly get the feeling that anybody was being watched or spied on.

Miss Pepper would lock up last thing before she went to bed; but as a matter of fact doors were often left unfastened all night at The Mills. It was a tight little community where everybody knew everybody and there were few strangers at any time, except Miss Studley's hand-picked guests. The surrounding woods belonged to large estates and were patrolled by game wardens, and at night the silence was vast and deep.

It was an odd little place, a settlement which had come into being a hundred years before almost by chance; the mills that named it were miles off and in ruins. It consisted of one long street, a back road that branched off from the Westbury road and rejoined the Westbury road to the north beyond a small place called Green Tree, which had not even a post office. There was almost no through traffic at all.

By twenty-five minutes past ten Mrs. Norbury was established on her sofa with a magazine, waiting for her massage and her iced cocoa. She wore a loose flowered dressing-gown, made so that it should at no point constrict her stout person; it was one of a series always in construction for her at a convent.

Her room was on the second floor in the rear, almost opposite the main stairway and near the head of another flight which led directly down to a side door. This door, like the others at Edgewood, had a screen, and like the others was often left open in hot weather for most of the night. It was open tonight, and the hall lights were unlighted; gnats did sometimes get into Edgewood; though The Mills was supposed to be free of them, and—according to old residents—was practically free of mosquitoes.

Mrs. Norbury's sofa was near the window, across the room from the door. She heard a faint sound from the direction of the door, looked up, and saw the knob slowly turning. The door was pushed open a little way. Then, as she watched it, expecting to see Miss Pepper and her tray (though Miss Pepper always knocked), it slowly and quietly closed.

Miss Pepper seemed to be acting in a peculiar way. Mrs. Norbury, slightly surprised, sat looking at the door. She called out: "Who's that?" but no one answered.

There was a slight eeriness about the whole thing. Mrs. Norbury got herself off her sofa, disentangled her feet from the long dressing-gown, and waddled to the door. She opened it and looked out.

She saw nothing in the dark hallway but the dim shapes of closed doors; but she thought she heard the screen at the foot of the side stairs close gently. She turned and gazed downwards. It was darker out than in, but she was sure that there was motion outside the screen; something moved away.

Mrs. Norbury, an intrepid old lady whose mind dealt almost exclusively with fact and who was annoyed by oddities, knew that anybody in Edgewood was free to take an evening stroll if he liked, and often did so; there were dry walks through the grounds, and one of them led around to the front drive. The garage was out there, and all the people in the house had cars except herself and Mrs. Turnbull, whose large impressive automobile was driven by a chauffeur; he had deposited Mrs. Turnbull at Edgewood and left, to return when she was ready to go. Jaunts to and from Pittsburgh were trifles in Mrs. Turnbull's philosophy of life.

But why should the person open Mrs. Norbury's door and retreat without explanation or apology? Every room had its private bath, even newcomers had no excuse for opening wrong doors. But Mrs. Turnbull was evidently a flighty person—except at bridge; her room was next door. She might have made the mistake, been too shy or ill-mannered to apologize, retreated in silence. Somebody else had gone out.

Since she couldn't explain the occurrence, and had learned from long experience that a great many occurrences had no rational explanation at all, but were the result of people's foolish impulses, Mrs. Norbury went back to her room and settled down again.

At half past ten Miss Pepper knocked and came in, bearing a jug of gratifying proportions on a tray. She was a brisk, freckled girl with many interests besides her job, and she was accustomed to minimize the alarms of the patients. She would not draw distinctions between the nervous system of Mrs. Norbury, for instance, and that of Mrs. Turnbull.

When Mrs. Norbury related her experience she said, to that lady's rage, that she had just imagined it.

"It? What?"

Miss Pepper had not been paying much attention. She put the tray down and looked vaguely at the door. "Perhaps the latch is loose."

"And the wind blew it open?" Mrs. Norbury fanned herself with her magazine.

"It's such an old house. They get warped."

Mrs. Norbury said distinctly: "Somebody opened my door and shut it again. This strong wind we have tonight wouldn't turn door handles. I never heard of a hurricane turning door handles."

Miss Pepper still thought that the whole thing was probably Mrs. Norbury's imagination. However, she said cheerfully: "If it worries you I could speak to Miss Studley. Would tomorrow do? She might be in bed."

Mrs. Norbury began to laugh. "If it was anywhere else," she chuckled, "know what I'd think? I'd think somebody came to pay a call on Mrs. Turnbull, and that I scared the life out of him."

Miss Pepper laughed too. "Try to scare up anything like that in Frazer's Mills!"

"Poor Miss Studley."

"She'd have a fit." Miss Pepper also was highly amused. She said: "*I* think somebody went out for a stroll and caught their sleeve on the knob going by. Look how loose the thing is."

14

2. AT THE LIBRARY

The Rigby Library in Frazer's Mills is next door to Edgewood, its grounds separated from the Edgewood grounds by an eight-foot hedge. This hedge stops short where the Rigby lawn turns into what used to be the Rigby kitchen gardens.

The Library is large for a place as small as Frazer's Mills, and if it were not the pride of the town, would be its white elephant. It had been donated, together with its books, by the last of the Rigbys, who had died many years before. The endowment no longer did more than pay taxes and repairs on it; The Mills now paid the librarian's salary and bought what new books it could. The house was a small but handsome brick building painted gray, with casement windows. Its front door, smothered in shrubbery, faced Edgewood. It had one large ground-floor room, lined to the ceiling with books—there had never been any reason for building stacks.

Miss Bluett, the librarian, was a native of Frazer's Mills, and had had no other job during the whole of her professional life. She had wanted no other. With what little money she had of her own, and her salary, she could live comfortably; she thought Frazer's Mills the most desirable place in the world, and she ran the Library as she chose.

At half past ten on Thursday night she was working late. There had been a local donation of books to the Library, she had had a chance to get them brought in that evening, and as she intended to start her Labor Day vacation on Friday morning she had decided to inspect and label the consignment beforehand; the Library Committee met the following week, and she didnt want to hurry with her report.

The books had been taken out of their boxes by Hawkins, the Library handy-man, and stacked around her desk. The desk was in a corner to the right of a back passage, diagonally across the room from the front door. Hawkins had left a narrow path for her between the piles of books.

Her desk lamp was on, the only light she needed. Several of the narrow casement windows were open for coolness, and so was the front door; but it had a screen. There was only one other door, the cellar entrance, which Hawkins kept locked because he had tools there.

At present Miss Bluett was down on her knees among the stacks of bound magazines, peering sideways at titles and muttering. She knew that the gift had all come out of the Carringtons' garret, and she was not particularly grateful for it. Most of it was battered, none of it was valuable so far as she could tell.

She heard a faint scratching or rattling somewhere behind her, thought vaguely of squirrels or luna moths—remarkable how much noise a big moth could make against a screen—and went on opening the big volumes of periodicals, one of which lay on her desk. The noise persisted. She looked over her shoulder at the screen door, and thought she saw the latch move. She had not fastened it, such a thing would never have occurred to her. She called out: "Who is it?"

She got no answer. The latch stopped moving, and something darker than shadow passed across the screen. She got to her feet.

The Library, isolated among its trees and well back from the street, was as quiet as death. Miss Bluett was far from nervous, nothing ever happened in The Mills to make people nervous; but the silence that had followed her question frightened her very much. She stood looking at the screen, and her throat was dry. There was

16

nothing to prevent the visitor from coming in, and she certainly couldn't get to the door first.

But a faint rustle from the rhododendrons to the right of the doorway told her that the visitor had departed. She waited a few moments, and then came to life. She strode to the light switch and turned it on; the ceiling bulbs flared. Then she snatched up a large red book from the nearest pile—it happened to be an old volume of *Who's Who* —and walked across to the door. She turned the handle of the screen, and found that it was locked after all.

Miss Bluett stood looking at it. She knew what had happened—the latch, like all the old fittings, was loose; it had locked itself when she closed the screen after her firmly, as she closed everything.

She wondered what the accident of the locked screen door had saved her from. She had not much imagination, but she couldn't help feeling that it had saved her from undesirable company. At any rate, whoever it was had apparently tried to get in, had failed, had not answered when she called out, and had gone quietly away. Miss Bluett did not propose to follow.

But it was one thing to be as frightened as she had been, another thing to admit it to others. Miss Bluett was a little tender of her own reputation for good sense. She did not wish the neighbors to tell her it had been a wandering dog or a wandering boy—there was only the Stapler boys, where she boarded—and to ask her if she had started looking for the burglar under the bed. Even with the perspiration of terror undried on her palms, Miss Bluett could not confess that she was afraid to go home alone.

She went back to her desk, sat down, and called up the Stapler house. She got Mrs. Stapler, and asked her if the boys were home, and if one of them could come for her with a flashlight. It was as dark as pitch out, and she had forgotten her own torch. "And I don't want to fall over myself the day before my vacation."

Mrs. Stapler said that Willie would be delighted. Miss

17

Bluett put her own torch in her desk drawer, and sat in the glare of the lights, looking at the doorway, until Willie came. She could not even shut and lock the front door— Willie might suspect why. Miss Bluett was a martyr to her own pride. Willie's piercing whistle, often an annoyance to her, was music in her ears.

Outside the door she paused. "I thought I heard a big dog around here, Willie. You see any place where he might have gone through those rhododendrons?"

Willie said they did look tore some.

3. AT THE WAKEFIELD INN

Between the old Rigby place and the more spacious Wakefield property to the south lies the Bay Horse Tavern. It is down on the street, only a narrow yard separating its porch from the footway; but behind it and up to the woods stretches a strip of wasteland overgrown with sumac, goldenrod and brambles, once the Tavern's stable yard and gardens.

The Tavern has no license to dispense liquors now, it is a tavern only in name; but it takes roomers upstairs, and its old sign—or a copy of it—hangs out below; a horse's head bridled. This is sentiment; the ground floor of the Tavern is given over to a drugstore, a general store and the post office.

Next door, well back from the street, is the fine old Wakefield house, now the Wakefield Inn. Miss Emeline Wakefield runs it as a select boardinghouse.

At about twenty minutes to eleven on Thursday night a young man, personable if rather bony as to form and features, sat up in bed at the Wakefield Inn, reading. He had arrived in his car at ten o'clock, and Miss Wakefield had told him at first, and firmly, that she had no room for him.

"I know you don't take transients," said the young man, who had ingratiating manners. "The Tavern said so when they sent me on. They're full up."

"Oh, yes," said Miss Wakefield. "I hear Mrs. Broadbent got those traveling salesmen who couldn't get rooms in Westbury on account of the Fair."

"Labor Day makes everything so crowded," said the

19

young man. "I'm only up for over Labor Day myself—up from New York. I have an uncle at Edgewood."

"Well, Mr. Yates, I don't think you would have been very comfortable at the Tavern. It's clean and decent, but very plain."

"And I understand it has no bar." Mr. Yates thought the tall, gaunt woman with the cropped hair who stood before him in the paneled hall looked like a sport; he spoke accordingly.

"The post office and general store are in the bar now," said Miss Wakefield. "Well, let's see. I could let you have Mr. Compson's room, I suppose. He's off for over the holiday, but you'll have to turn out on Monday evening."

"That would be—"

"I can only let you have it because he always expects me to deduct his board and lodging while he's away on his trips. I don't know why I should keep the room empty."

"Neither do I."

"Several other guests are away too, but they don't want any reductions. I don't know what's got into Tom Compson, he has plenty of money, but he's getting very close in his old age. They say people do."

"I've heard so."

"You'll have to be very careful of his things."

"I will, you can trust me."

"The man's gone home. Mind driving around to the garage and putting your car up? You'll find a place. Hope you don't feel unequal to lugging your own bag."

Mr. Yates laughed and said he didn't.

"I'll wait here for you."

Yates went and got his bag out of the car and brought it up to the porch. Then he drove around to the back and found the garage; the only lights anywhere came from his own lamps. He pushed open the garage door and got the car in. He walked back to the house through a mist that was almost rain.

Miss Wakefield had towels over her arm. She led him

through a large room on the left to a side hall, and into a corner room opposite.

"Quietest room in the house," she said. "Used to be the library. It's cut off from the back premises by a little cross passage, as you see, and the back stairs are just beyond. There's no bathroom down here, I'm sorry to say, but there's one just at the head of the back stairs. It's a regular bachelor's room. Side door to the garden along the passage, makes you quite independent." She arranged the towels on an old-fashioned rack. "I know how men are, and a lot of women too; they hate always running into other boarders and having to say things about the weather fifty times a day."

Yates, looking at the big double bed, said the room was a perfect paradise.

Miss Wakefield turned down the bed. "Breakfast at nine, I mean it stops after that." She turned to face him. "You look a little tired."

"Nothing at all, I feel fine." Yates managed to look pathetic. "I suppose I couldn't have a cup of coffee in bed?"

"We haven't full service by any means, but you're on the dining-room floor. You can have a tray in your room. Everybody could while we had proper service."

"If it wouldn't be too much trouble I'd like that."

"I like it myself. Well, might as well enjoy yourself. You haven't brought golf clubs?"

"No, I didn't think I'd get any golf."

"Oh well, if you want to play I suppose they can fix you up at the Westbury Club."

Yates, glancing about him, said he saw that Mr. Compson played chess.

"Yes. Terrible game, isn't it? I never could see it. Haven't the brains. Goodnight, and I hope you'll be comfortable."

"Awfully good of you to take me in."

"I suppose there's stuff to read here." Miss Wakefield looked round her with the faintly hostile air of one to whom reading is an enemy of outdoor games and healthy

21

exercise. Yates, glancing at Mr. Compson's stack of magazines, said he would find something.

Miss Wakefield left him. He unpacked his bag, and then in shirtsleeves, and with his towel over his arm and his toilet case in his hand, made the journey to the bathroom. He met nobody. On his way back he looked along the cross passage to the open, screened door that Miss Wakefield had spoken of.

"Privacy, all right," he told himself. "Compson could live his own life."

He went down the hallway to his room. It had a big bow window facing the front, but no side windows. However, plenty of damp fresh air came in, quite enough.

He got into bed, picked up a magazine from the night table, and settled down.

A slight fumbling noise caused him to look up and across to the door. The handle of the door moved gently. But more from habit than from any other reason, Yates had turned the key; the door therefore did not open. Wondering whether Mr. Compson had returned unexpectedly, and hoping not, he called: "What's wanted?"

The ensuing silence puzzled him. But he was not acquainted with the ways of the Inn, somebody thinking the room empty might have come down for matches or reading matter or something. There was a slightly furtive effect, however, in the whole thing—the way the handle had turned, the quiet withdrawal afterwards. Yates got out of bed.

Remembering in time that he didn't wear pajamas, he put on a bathrobe and slippers and went across to the door. He opened it and looked out; nothing.

He crossed to the opposite door and listened; no sound in the lounge or drawing room, and none, when he reached them, on the back stairs. There was a further door leading to the rear of the house, but he didn't open it; his attention had been caught and fixed by something on the floor at the foot of the stairs, something that just caught the faint light from his room.

He had barely noticed it before; it had hung in a niche,

22

above a shelf on which stood two buckets; one full of sand, one full of water. He bent over and picked it up—a short fire axe.

Mr. Yates stood contemplating it and chewing his lower lip. He looked up at the brackets it had hung on; it simply couldn't have fallen. By no stretch of the imagination could it be fitted into normal activity of any sort. It fitted rather well, he uneasily thought, with that lunatic fumbling at his door; and he felt a certain relief at the fact that that door had happened to be locked.

Mr. Yates found himself in something of a quandary. Musing, he half turned and looked to his left along the cross passage on which he stood to the screen door at the end of it, beyond which there was utter darkness. But he did not think of it as a way of retreat; it somehow never occurred to him that the lunatic had come from outside.

He reached a conclusion. Much as he would have preferred to hang the axe on its brackets and go back to his room and to bed, he simply couldn't do it. Nothing for it, he must convey his odd information to Miss Wakefield.

He put the axe down where he had found it, then shook his head angrily and took it into his room. He crossed to the lounge opposite, made his way to the front hall, and found a light switch. He went up the broad stairs to an upper hall, where closed doors confronted him. He raised his voice: "Miss Wakefield? Miss Wa-a-kefield."

Heads appeared in doorways. One of them was tied up in a bath towel and dripped soapsuds; another, with rumpled hair, belonged to a scholarly-looking middle-aged man with pince-nez; a third appeared behind his shoulder, feminine and frightened. Three pairs of eyes looked at Yates as if he had come through the roof.

"It's all right," he said. "I'm Miss Wakefield's transient. Nothing's wrong, I just want to speak to her."

The scared woman asked: "You didn't smell smoke, did you?"

"No, I assure you I didn't."

Miss Wakefield came out of a room at the end of the hall. She had a blue net on her hair, and for a dressing-gown she wore a raincoat tightly belted. She asked: "Want something, Mr. Yates?"

"Could I speak to you a minute?"

"Come in."

The heads disappeared. They think I have a stomach ache, thought Yates, and followed Miss Wakefield into a large front room.

"Awfully sorry to come up and bawl for you like that," he said, "but I couldn't see any way out of it. I didn't want to knock at doors. Hoped I wouldn't wake anybody."

"That's all right. What is it?"

"Something I thought you ought to know about. Anyhow, I couldn't let it go without putting it up to you."

"What in the world is it?"

"Perhaps it would be better if you came downstairs—the back way."

Miss Wakefield followed him along the hall, and then took the lead around a corner and down the back stairs. He showed her the empty brackets where the axe had hung and related his experience. When he had finished she stood gazing at him, flabbergasted. At last she asked: "Where is it?"

"I thought I'd better put it away in my room. Of course there may not be anything in all this; you may have some idea—"

"I haven't any idea at all."

"Somebody wouldn't have been chopping kindling and left the axe—"

"It's never been touched since the fire warden put it up five years ago."

Yates smiled at her. "I'm afraid you think I'm the lunatic, Miss Wakefield."

"Certainly I don't."

"I assure you I'd rather have gone back to bed."

"You had to tell me, of course. It wasn't anybody in the house, Mr. Yates. I've known all these people forever. The Silvers and their boy are all together in their room and Dick's sleeping porch. Miss Homans was washing her hair—spoke to me about an extra towel only a minute ago."

"Servants?"

"They're all local help, and they sleep at home—farms or the village. Those four upstairs are the only guests I have at present—as I told you, the rest are off for over Labor Day." Miss Wakefield looked over her shoulder at the screen door behind her. "We never had prowlers."

"Er—could one get in?"

"I suppose so. You may think it's funny, but half the time we don't lock up. People in and out. My soul."

"The trouble is it all seems a little *crazy*."

Miss Wakefield glanced about her and up the back stairs. "My soul, he might be still in the house."

"We'll soon find out, if you like."

"Would you? I'll come too."

"Just to direct me. Stay well behind."

"Hadn't you better take something? I mean the axe."

"I might use it as a club, I suppose. The prowler doesn't seem very effectual. Easily discouraged."

"Thank goodness you locked your door. I suppose I ought to tell the others, but I hate to upset them. And Dickie Silver would simply revel in it. Such a fuss."

"If we search the house and don't find anybody we can lock up and be all right till tomorrow."

Yates went and got the axe. Then he and Miss Wakefield went through the house, very quietly, from attics to cellar. They found nobody.

"Just as I thought," said Yates, locking the side door. "He left as he came—this way."

Miss Wakefield stood frowning. "If we only had a constable. There's nobody nearer than Westbury, the state police are beyond that. I mean it wouldn't be fair not to notify people, would it? Perhaps we ought to have done that first."

"Can't think of everything at once," said Yates, whose heart was sinking.

"I could call Edgewood, and the Tavern, and the Carringtons. That ought to be enough— Mrs. Broadbent would send out and tell the neighbors. It isn't late, that's one thing."

Yates looked at his wrist watch. "No, only ten fifty-five plus. I suppose we aren't making too much of this, Miss Wakefield? I mean it's only what I noticed, and this confounded thing." He looked at the axe in his hand. "And I've got fingerprints all over it. That was bright of me."

"Well, at least the man didn't take it. That's funny, too, isn't it? Some crazy person. We really ought to telephone."

Yates gloomily agreed.

They went through to the front hall, where Miss Wakefield, her voice kept low, called Edgewood. While she was waiting for an answer she talked to Yates:

"This is a funny little place, you know. It isn't a quarter of a mile long, the whole thing, and just this one street. Edgewood at one end, Carringtons' at the other, on this side. On the other . . . Yes, Miss Studley? This is Emeline Wakefield. I thought I ought to tell you there's been a prowler around. . . . Yes, got in here through the side door and then left. Somebody heard him. . . . Well, I don't understand it myself. He seems to have taken down the fire axe and then left it. You might lock up, if you haven't already. . . . That's all right."

She turned to Yates. "Miss Studley doesn't scare easy. Well, now for the Tavern."

As she waited for the Tavern to answer, Yates, leaning against the telephone table with the axe dangling from one listless hand, said he hadn't realized Frazer's Mills was so small.

"Sixty souls at present, counting the farms to the west. Don't you know how The Mills was settled? . . . Oh, Mrs. Broadbent, I called up to say that there's some kind of crazy tramp wandering around tonight. . . . No, he wasn't seen. Just heard." Miss Wakefield cast a look at the axe. With the receiver to her ear, she addressed Yates in a whisper: "No use getting the whole town up here tonight, overrunning us." She answered Mrs. Broadbent's voluble comments: "I'll tell you all about it in the morning. Just at present we ought to let the place know. I'm calling the Carringtons. Could you send down the street, and perhaps notify the farms?"

Mrs. Broadbent talked for some time.

"That's nice of you," replied Miss Wakefield. "I've called Edgewood. I haven't anybody here to send out, and it would take so long to telephone. . . . I can't imagine either where he came from."

She put down the receiver. "The whole village will get it in the next few minutes. Just a row of cottages, you know, across the way, and the girls' school is closed and the housekeeper's in New York getting supplies she won't be back till morning."

The Carrington house answered promptly to her ring.

"That you, Lawrence? How's your father? . . . That's good." Miss Wakefield told her story for the third time, but this hearer seemed bent upon details. Miss Wakefield supplied them. "Yes, he did get in. . . . My transit heard him and found the axe on the floor." She scowled. "Mr. Yates, a very nice fellow. Don't bother about him. . . . Yes, I thought of the state police, but . . . All right, if you want to. I know that's what they're for, it's only that I didn't want them roaring through and waking the whole village. . . . Well, thanks, Lawrence. Don't scare Lydia."

She hung up. "That's Lawrence Carrington for you, always so fussy. And now where shall we put that thing?"

They settled on a store cupboard in the rear front hall. Miss Wakefield locked the axe up and took the key.

Yates, instead of retiring to his room, stood looking at her. She returned the look inquiringly.

"Miss Wakefield, I've been a damn fool."

"You certainly have not."

"The whole thing may turn out to be nothing at all some harmless half-wit walking in his sleep."

"Well, he'd have to walk a long way, because there are none in the place, unless Miss Studley has one at Edgewood. And she never takes people like that."

Yates made a face. "Don't talk about Edgewood."

27

"Why not?"

"Miss Wakefield, I have no uncle there."

"You haven't?"

"I don't know a soul in the place. I've never been here in my life before, and if I'd known it was such a small place I'd never have told you that whopper. I thought Edgewood was somewhere on the outskirts, like most sanatoriums; but Frazer's Mills seems to *be* an outskirt."

Miss Wakefield, frowning severely, kept her prominent blue eyes on him. "Well, what was the idea?"

"The idea was that I thought you'd let me stay here if I had some kind of local reference. I couldn't get in anywhere in Westbury on account of the Fair, and they told me to try the Bay Horse Tavern in Frazer's Mills. The Tavern sent me on to you—I didn't realize that this wasn't a regular inn. I was tired, and I didn't want to drive back to New York tonight. So I invented Uncle at Edgewood, and if it hadn't been for the prowler—"

Miss Wakefield said: "Now you think the state police may come around checking up on everybody—out-of-town people."

"They certainly will."

"But you came and told me."

"Hang it, I'm the only witness. They'll check up on me, all right."

She studied him. "You needn't have said a word."

"About the prowler? That would have been a nice return for your kindness, wouldn't it?"

"What are you up here in this neighborhood for, anyway?"

"Just touring. Holiday trip. But I don't think I'd better go on with it if I have no better luck getting rooms than I had at Westbury. Miss Wakefield, I have perfectly good references in New York. My family's in California, but you can call up any number of people."

She said: "I'd better have a look at your driving license and so on."

They went to Mr. Compson's room, and Yates supplied her with a wad of papers, including a bill for club dues, his checkbook, and certain records reminiscent of the late war, which established one Garston Yates as ex-captain in the Air Force.

"All right," said Miss Wakefield.

"You mean you won't tell them about my uncle at Edgewood?"

She burst out laughing, and after a pause Yates laughed too, but restrainedly.

4. AT THE CARRINGTONS'

At about ten minutes to eleven something hardly more visible than a shadow made its way towards the Carrington house from the north. The grounds here, on the side next to the Wakefield Inn, were rough and thickly planted with old trees; the house itself was almost hidden by its maples, and apparently quite dark.

A little gleam like a firefly appeared and disappeared in front of the moving shadow, never showing for more than a moment at a time. It vanished and did not reappear when the shadow rounded the house and mounted the front steps. No light here in any window, and the front door stood open on a dark hall. The shadow crossed the porch, hesitated, and went softly in. There were no screens at the Carringtons'.

Five minutes later the dark shape came out again, descended the steps, and moved to the right. The firefly danced again, farther and farther away, up the south lawn; then it was no longer to be seen.

At twelve minutes past eleven Lawrence Carrington, in the library at the back of the house, put down the telephone and looked at his sister Lydia. She had just come in from the dining room, carrying a night-light, a sort of shaded candle, in her hand.

Carrington, a slight, blond man of forty or more, was frowning a little. He said: "That was Emeline Wakefield."

"What in the world does she want at this hour?"

"She says there's been a prowler at the Inn."

"A what?"

"The prowler, the prowler. Made you nervous."

"I'd rather like to call Emeline and find out what really happened. There's a boy there with his family— that Silver boy. He might have been playing around with that axe. It's too bad to get the state police here and make a fuss if there *is* no prowler."

"Some transient of Emeline's worked her up."

"Transient? At the Inn? What next?"

Lawrence said: "I don't know. Very much better to call the barracks if there's any chance—" He glanced down at a chessboard on the table, and moved a piece. Then he moved it back again. He said: "She's got me."

"Rose has?"

"What a question! Who else is the expert here? I won-der if there's profit in professional chess."

"I'm glad she's to have the attic. She ought to have a place of her own to entertain in and play her radio."

"Here? Whom can she entertain in Frazer's Mills? Well, the books are all out, anyhow. That last lot going tomorrow?"

"Oh, I didn't tell you. Hattie Bluett sent Hawkins for them at seven o'clock, and there were some in Father's room, and I actually had to creep in and collect them for Hawkins."

"You mean you let Hattie Bluett make you go in and get books away from Father while he was asleep? He will be pleased."

"He was just looking some old things over; things he liked when he was a boy. He won't care."

"You let the whole village order you about."

"Well, you know Hattie."

"She's in a class by herself, and so is The Mills."

"She wants to go off on a bus trip tomorrow over Labor Day, and she wanted to have a full report for the committee on Tuesday. They're raising money or some-thing."

"They'd better. Our Library is an anachronism. It'll die with Hattie Bluett. She'll be found disintegrating among the ruins."

"She takes it so seriously. She does love it so when she can collect a fine."

She sat down near him. He looked up at her. "You're tired. I wonder how much you do around the house, now that we have nobody sleeping in."

"Nothing at all."

"You've been upstairs all evening, haven't you? There was no light in your sitting room."

"I've been upstairs; writing out checks."

"Why don't you get in a nurse for Father when he has rheumatism?"

"Nurse? He doesn't need one. He gets about. He'd loathe a nurse."

"I bet he would. You're in and out waiting on him a dozen times an hour, and Rose Jenner doesn't lift a finger. You ought to get somebody extra from the village, somebody he knows—"

"You find the somebody, Lawrence."

A bell tinkled sweetly. Lawrence said: "There she is at last," and went through to the front door. He opened it. A young girl stood on the threshold, dark hair in a long thick bang over her forehead. She wore a thin raincoat thrown back from her yellow sweater and skirt. She said: "Why all shut up on a night like this?"

"Sh. Your guardian's asleep."

"Still?" Picking up the lantern, she came into the house.

"Yes, thank goodness."

She followed him back into the library, pushing damp hair back and shrugging out of her coat. She had a wide forehead, yellowish eyes, a wide mouth with a full underlip. She gave the impression of great beauty, although not a single feature taken alone could account for the effect.

She stood in the library doorway. "Finish the problem?" she asked, looking at the chessboard.

"No, and I don't believe you can."

"Ha! Want to go on struggling, or shall I show you?"

"Time enough tomorrow."

"How was the movie, Rose?" asked Lydia.

"All right. I was out by eleven, but I had trouble getting the car out."

Lydia said: "You mustn't drive about so late again until they find the prowler."

"The what, Lydia?"

"Miss Wakefield says there's a crazy person about. She called up a little while ago."

"Is that why you locked up?"

"That's why." Lawrence was again at the chessboard. Rose Jenner stood looking at him and then at Lydia. She said: "I don't understand about this prowler."

"Don't worry, the state police are coming. Lawrence sent for them," said Lydia.

"But is it a tramp? How did Miss Wakefield find out about him?"

Lawrence rather wearily and sketchily explained.

"You mean she called up right away?"

Lydia said: "She'd already called Edgewood and Mrs. Broadbent, hadn't she, Lawrence?"

"So she said. So I told them at the barracks."

"And then she called you, and then you locked the front door?"

"And the cellar door, and the kitchen door, and the back door." Lawrence looked up at her. "Did we do right, please?"

Lydia said: "Only the back door was shut. The others were—"

Rose turned and started out of the room. Lydia asked: "What's the matter?"

Rose looked over her shoulder. "I just want to see whether my guardian's all right."

Lawrence half got to his feet. "All right! What do you mean?"

"It only takes a minute or so to get here from the Wakefield Inn."

Lydia sprang up. "I listened. I was afraid of waking him." But Rose had gone. The brother and sister exchanged blank looks.

Lawrence said, sharp anxiety now in his voice: "She's

35

so imaginative. Almost unbalanced. Don't be frightened, it's nonsense."

"I never thought."

"Why should you?" But he made for the door. Lydia was close behind him when they met Rose coming out of the dark parlor. They could barely see one another's faces by the shaded glow of the lantern held in her left hand. Her eyes, normally half closed, were wide open; her features expressionless.

She said: "I can't wake him. There was a log of wood on the floor." Extending her right hand, she held it out. "There's blood on it."

5. PSYCHOLOGICAL

The young man at the filling station counted out Gamadge's change. He asked: "You hear about the murder?"

"Murder?"

"You're headed for Frazer's Mills. I thought—"

The filling station was at a cross-road. Gamadge had in fact turned his car off the Westbury route, pointing it east. He said: "I thought this branch went to a place called Green Tree."

The young man looked dashed. He said: "It goes to Green Tree, all right, but you have to pass Frazer's Mills. Didn't you hear about the murder?"

"That's so, I read something in the paper. I didn't realize that Frazer's Mills was along here. I suppose there isn't a cordon or anything?"

"Say, it happened Thursday night. This is Sunday. All over, except they didn't catch the maniac. I thought you might be from a newspaper."

"No, I'm not." Gamadge tipped the man and put the rest of the change in his pocket. "I just follow this dirt road, do I?"

"That's it, no forks except farm tracks and an old road to the pond."

"Thanks." Gamadge drove off between rolling fields full of stacked corn and pumpkins. A mile on he stopped at a lunch wagon and asked for a cup of coffee.

The man handed it through the car window. "Come about the murder?"

"Murder?"

"The atrocity at Frazer's Mills."

"Oh, sure enough, I go through Frazer's Mills. I'm headed for Green Tree."

"Oh well, I guess the curiosity seekers are about through by this time. I'll be moving back to the route in time for the holiday tomorrow."

"Isn't this your usual pitch?"

"Wouldn't get any trade here from one year to another. But you never saw such traffic as we had since Thursday night, durn near tore the old road up. That's why they never made a good one, I guess the wagon trade stopped when the old mills did."

Gamadge drank his coffee, handed the cup back to the man, and paid. He started his engine. "Are they still saying it was a maniac?"

"What else can they say? He tried to get into three or four other houses first. Them monsters don't always get caught, the papers said."

"Not for a long time, if they once get clear."

"They say they're just like anybody else, in between-times."

"So I've heard."

"The state police let me have a gun."

"That's right."

Gamadge drove on; thick woods now pressed down upon the road at the right, and a stream made itself heard just beyond the roadway. He drove slowly, enjoying the warmth and fragrance of late summer.

A rutted track branched off to his right, and (forgetful it seemed of the filling-station man's warning) he turned into it. It sloped gently upwards. Trees on both sides of him now; the morning sun came through in patterns that moved on the road. He climbed to a ridge. Below, and some distance away, two ruined stone buildings stood beside a millpond. A bridge crossed the dam; beyond it stood a car, and on the steep bank of the pond a young man waited. He waved an arm.

Gamadge coasted down, stopped his car and got out. The young man came to meet him. He said: "Gamadge, this is pretty kind of you."

"Well, Garry, your call sounded like an S.O.S."

"It was. Come on over here and let's sit down."

They sat on a fallen log above the bank; Gamadge lighted a cigarette and leaned forward, elbows on his knees. He looked out across the quiet waters of the pond. "Nice up here," he said.

Yates glanced at him, aware of an unexpected failure in self-confidence. He had known Gamadge all his life, had played as a child in the Gamadge library, twirling the terrestrial and the celestial globes and building bridges out of books, while Gamadge was a schoolboy and Gamadge's parents still alive. Later, when the house had been partly remodeled into office, darkroom and laboratory, and Gamadge had set up for himself as book and document expert, Yates had not seen so much of him; and during the past eight years, when he had applied his consideration of old texts and newer forgeries of them to life and the ways of mankind, had practised criminology and warred with murder, Yates had not seen him at all.

Gamadge had married and acquired a son, had served in a far from publicized capacity in the war. He had taken part in some dozen police investigations. Had all this changed him? Yates remembered him as an easygoing, amusing character, quite unassertive, a good listener; cool-headed at bridge and golf. Clever, of course; he had written some brilliant little books; but had Yates underestimated a personality which now struck the young man as obscurely formidable, certainly to be reckoned with?

Hindsight, perhaps. Gamadge had responded immediately to Yates' call, and whatever else he might be he was still casual in manner and without much apparent ego: a green-eyed, tallish man, well-dressed, easy mannered, a little stooped from his sedentary occupation.

He now asked, looking over his shoulder, "Those the mills?"

"Grist and saw. They didn't really name the place, you know."

"No?"

"The place was just a few scattered farms at first, had no name; then when these people came here and settled they called it Frazer's Mills just to call it something."

"I gathered that the settlement came into being more or less by accident."

"Yes, it did. Five or six families—sporting characters—had their horses and training stables and so on up here, handy for the Westbury races. They liked the place, and they all built country-houses—sort of rich men's hobby. Land was cheap a hundred years ago, though. The gardeners and stablemen and so on had cottages, and their descendants live in the cottages now. It's a backwater and it never developed; nobody wanted it to."

"Sounds delightful." Gamadge dreamily smoked, listening to the water gurgling over the broken dam. "Lovely place, anyhow."

"Yes, it is. I wish I'd known more about its peculiarities before I made such an ass of myself here. But I couldn't know there was going to be a murder, and I didn't happen to know that the place was nothing but one street, with that rest-cure place right on it."

"Here's a piece of sound advice from an old campaigner, Garry my boy. Always act as if there were going to be a murder. Then——"

Yates showed irritation. "Yes, I know. What a wonderful time we'd all have."

Gamadge cast a sidelong look at the glum profile of his companion. He asked cheerfully: "Well, what's the trouble, apart from your having to stick around in this nice part of the country until after the Carrington inquest?"

"To begin with, I told Miss Wakefield at the Inn that I had an uncle at Edgewood. That was so she'd take me as a transient, but I think she'd have taken me anyway. It was a kind of joke, I suppose," said Yates gloomily. "It more or less slipped out, I don't know why; I thought Edgewood was off somewhere, never imagined she'd check up or know."

"I think it was the damndest silly——"

"Never mind what you think; I think so too. It didn't really matter, because as soon as we had the prowler incident, and you certainly read about all that in the papers—"

"I did."

"Well, I knew there'd be a checkup if the state police got into it, so I beat them to it and told Miss Wakefield that I was there on false pretenses. She's a wonderful sport—descended from an original settler and rides an enormous bay horse—he's a descendant of original stock too. The local gentry built themselves and their retainers a tavern, wasn't that an idea? *The Bay Horse.* Somewhere to go of an evening, I suppose, get away from their families and play checkers and swap news—and bet on their favorites. Their breeding-stable specialty was these bays. Well, Miss Wakefield saw the point, that I was just trying to get a lodging for the night; there's a fair at Westbury, you know, and holiday crowds everywhere. The Tavern, which is now a boardinghouse upstairs and the post office and drugstore beneath—it was full of traveling salesmen. By the way, they were playing poker on Thursday evening, and they've been allowed to go."

Gamadge said he was glad of it, poor devils.

"I showed my credentials to Miss Wakefield," continued Yates, "and the nice old girl agreed to say nothing to anybody about my whopper. Everything would have been all right, but then came this ghastly murder at the Carringtons'—next door. There are two big lawns between, but it's no distance away."

Gamadge said: "I don't know how on earth they could involve you in it, if that's your trouble. You can prove you were at the Inn by the merest accident, can't you?"

"Yes, the Tavern and the places I tried in Westbury back me up there."

"And even if you'd had time to get to the Carringtons' and back after Miss Wakefield settled you in your room and before you called her about the prowler—"

"I had, of course."

"You can't have had time to make those other visits

first—at Edgewood and the Library. As I remember it, the Edgewood call was at about ten twenty-five, the Library call at ten thirty. You got to the Inn at ten o'clock, and you must have talked to Miss Wakefield for a while, arguing your way in."

"And putting up my car. It was well after ten twenty-five when she left me."

"Well then. Everybody's agreed that there was only one prowler that night, there really couldn't have been more. Homicidal maniacs don't come in threes."

Yates looked at him. *"You* think it's psychological, then."

"Think it's what?"

"Think it's a maniac."

"I don't think anything. I spoke according to general opinion. It looks like a psychopathological crime."

"It has to be. There's no motive. There can't be one."

"So I gather from what the newspapers say. They haven't gone into details."

"I know the details. There's no possible sane connection between old Mrs. Norbury at Edgewood, and Miss Bluett, the librarian, and old Mr. Compson or me, and Carrington."

"Well, as I say, even a maniac can't be in two places at once, and even a maniac—this kind of maniac—doesn't go out of his way to call attention to his own crime." Gamadge dropped the end of his cigarette and ground it out under his heel. "So what's your trouble, and why did you get me up here at great personal inconvenience and in distress of mind on your account? I thought I'd find that you had an important private date on Tuesday, and wanted to get out of attending the inquest. I wouldn't put it past you. What I can't understand is why you were so determined to stay in Frazer's Mills that night. It's only a two hour and a half run to New York. What were you doing up here anyway?"

Yates picked up a flat stone and skipped it across the pond to an island of lily-pads. He watched the ripples broaden in its wake. "That's the trouble," he said. "I didn't tell Miss Wakefield that. I haven't told anybody. But they may find out. I came up to see Rose Jenner."

Gamadge whistled softly between his teeth. This exasperated Mr. Yates to violence.

"She's a wonderful girl, I never met such a girl. It isn't our fault that I've been seeing her on the quiet. The Carringtons don't like her friends. She does collect some queer ones, but that's because she likes intelligent people —I'm the only low-brow she ever bothered with. We thought it would be a good plan for me to come up over Labor Day and stay in the neighborhood, so that we could see something of each other and drive around the back country. We met in Westbury at a roadhouse—she told them she was going to a movie. We thought we'd better not come back here together—I tried to get a room at Westbury and couldn't, so she suggested the Tavern here. I came along first. She went to the movie, the end of it, so she'd be able to say what it was about, and get home at the right time. I haven't seen her since, I haven't dared to telephone, I don't know what happened; I suppose there was a big crowd that night, and that's why nobody saw her go in—I mean nobody remembers it. If she left by the side exit, as she says, nobody'd see her go out. Of course she'd worry about her guardian when she realized from what the others said that the maniac had had time to get across to the house from the Wakefield Inn. She was fond of Carrington. Why shouldn't she go in and investigate? That's what Lawrence and Miss Carrington ought to have done."

The rush of words ended at last, and there was a silence. When Gamadge spoke it was mildly:

"Let me try to understand all this. I gathered from the newspapers that Miss Jenner, for all anybody seemed to know, might have come home much earlier from Westbury, and driven in by way of Green Tree; or she might never have gone to Westbury at all. The papers simply left that to be inferred, and they implied that she seemed convinced, when she did get home, that something had happened to George Carrington. They didn't make much of either suggestion, and they seem to think that there was no financial motive for anybody's killing him."

"There is none. Nobody but a maniac can have killed him, and for that matter nobody but a maniac would have risked those other calls—at Edgewood and the Library and the Inn. He might easily have been caught coming or going. I'd have caught him myself, if I'd had my wits about me."

"That's true, you might."

"And why *make* those other calls, if the object of the whole thing was George Carrington's murder? It was some kind of maniac, that's absolutely sure."

"But not a case of acute mania; we can rule that out."

Yates looked at him keenly. "Because there was all that creeping around beforehand?"

"It must have been beforehand; no time for it after the murder. And rudimentary precautions taken, like that blurring of footprints on the Carrington steps and porch."

"Something tied over the fellow's shoes." Yates mused grimly.

"Well." Gamadge sat up, took out his cigarette case, chose a cigarette, and lighted it. "You came up here and met Miss Jenner at this roadhouse. For reasons not quite clear to me, your friendship with her was a secret; after all, you're presentable."

"But I can't support her yet. I'm only just able to support myself. I couldn't start in on anything until this year, like everybody else my age who went to war."

"Still—but we'll return to that. I suppose you had made these efforts to find a place to stay in Westbury before you met her at the roadhouse?"

"Yes. So she suggested the Tavern here."

"You arrived at the Wakefield Inn, and you made a mystery of yourself."

"There was no reason to tell Miss Wakefield that I was here to see Rose Jenner. Every reason why I shouldn't. And after the murder it would only have meant big extra publicity for her—I don't matter, I don't care about myself. It wouldn't hurt me, anyhow."

"But you think it may come out—that you know her, and that you met her at the roadhouse on Thursday evening when she was supposed to be at a movie in Westbury?"

"It might come out any time," said Yates drearily. "Her picture's in all the papers—she found the body. Mine may be in the papers too, after that inquest."

"Well, what of it?"

"What of it?" Yates met his eyes; they exchanged a long look.

"Yes, what of it? Extra publicity won't hurt Miss Jenner. Discovery of a love interest—you—won't hurt her. If she had none she'd be—er—exceptional. How old is she?"

"Nineteen."

"You say there was no financial motive for Carrington's murder, and we agree—with everybody else—that it wasn't and couldn't have been a case of acute mania—sudden brainstorm, result of a quarrel, result of goodness knows what. What did you expect me to do for you —or her?"

Yates said without looking at him: "I thought you might find out somehow who this maniac really is, or where to find him. They're digging up all kinds of stuff about Rose's father. He was erratic, she had a tough time when she was a child. They lived in Europe—did I say?—knocked around, no money. When she was ten years old he had her playing in exhibition chess matches. He was an amateur champion himself, and he taught her."

Gamadge said nothing.

"They say chess has an awful history," said Yates somberly.

"Chess masters do go off their heads now and then."

"She hates chess," exclaimed Yates. "Hates it. Always did."

"No wonder."

"She never plays, except when the Carringtons want a game. Of course she's right out of their class. She says she's really not much good at it, not since she stopped being a prodigy; but that's just her way of talking—she hates it so."

"Did her father die insane, Yates?"

"She says not; but he drank and I think took some drug."

"What relation is she to the Carringtons?"

"None at all, not even adopted. Her mother died when she was only a few years old, and then George Carrington's older daughter married Jenner, one of those infatuations, very much against her father's wish. After she died—Rose said they really didn't have the necessities of life then—Rose and her father lived together alone. The war was on, and they'd been in Switzerland. When she was fifteen he died too, and some friends wrote to Carrington that she was practically destitute, and enclosed a letter her stepmother had left for him, asking him to take care of Rose."

"Must have been fond of the child."

"They were devoted; Rose thinks all the Carringtons are perfect. Carrington got her over here somehow, and he's looked out for her ever since. Sent her to a good school, wanted her to go to college. You see he had nothing to leave her."

"I don't see, you haven't explained."

"In nineteen thirty-two he put everything he had into an annuity. It gave him a fine income, and his son and daughter approved—they have some money of their own from their mother. But they'll never be able to live in the same style now. They had every reason for wanting him to live forever, and he more or less intended to."

"I'm beginning to understand the situation. The papers haven't gone into it."

"No, because nobody can suspect the Carringtons of murdering him. Even if they weren't fond of him, they had every reason, as I said, for keeping him alive. They have the house, I think, but Rose—she told me all this— Rose says land isn't valuable up here at present, and the house isn't even wired for electricity; needs everything. It wouldn't bring much. The Edgewood property and the old Compson house—where the school is now—went for a song."

"Miss Jenner thinks the Carringtons are perfect, but she had to see her friends secretly?"

"She didn't have to. You ought to understand that she was brought up to be absolutely independent, and here she feels tied down. It was a middle-aged household, and she felt that her friends were a disturbance; and some mighty queer ones she did collect. And Carrington had this horror of bad marriages—on account of this other daughter of his, Jenner's wife, and because he had no money to leave. And not much to give, either; he was the greatest spender on earth, Rose said; she thought it was wonderful of him to spend so much on her school and give her an allowance."

"She didn't want to present an admirer who couldn't afford to marry out of hand?"

"I wasn't very anxious to be taken there and looked over, I must admit. I suppose it was adventure, to meet on the quiet."

"Carrington couldn't have stopped the marriage."

"Of course not, she's of age to marry. In two years I may be making decent money."

"When did you meet her?"

"Last Christmas holidays, in a bar. She liked to go off by herself, away from the Carringtons' formal existence, and see life. She isn't wild, Gamadge; for instance she drinks like a civilized European, not the way we pour it down. Her father was a cultivated man, I'll say that for him. Next winter, if she decided against college and tried for a job, the Carringtons were going to introduce her socially. She hated the idea. So did I. I might have lost her. I'm not much, and she might have found somebody she liked better. Gamadge—I'm not giving you the right impression of her. She's never criticized these people. She was delighted when Carrington had that attic cleared out for her—the attic the books came from that Miss Bluett was working on late on Thursday night. After all, it's pleasanter to have a place of your own. Rose isn't a secretive type at all. Can't you understand that when you're her age and been on your own, you don't want a lot of questions? Carrington felt responsible for her, and he was old-fashioned, and he asked a lot of questions."

"She seems to have had liberty and the use of a car."

"She's a natural with cars, and these roads were always safe until now."

"Did she ever tell you anything about her own mother?"

"Hardly remembers her. She was from Budapest, but part English. On the stage, I think."

"Jenner was an American?"

"Yes, expatriate. Lived in Paris till the war. He'd had money, but he'd spent it. No profession. I'm afraid he lived by his wits after his first wife died."

"She supported him?"

"I suppose so. He may have thought Carrington's daughter would have money."

"He sounds a little as though he ought to have been boiled in oil." Gamadge was remembering a scene from his own past—a hollow square within which a very small pale boy walked from chess table to chess table, glancing at each for a moment, putting out a delicate little hand to move a piece or to castle, passing on. Afterwards he had looked like collapsing, but members of the club had wanted autographs and the father had made him write them.

"She can't bear to talk about her chess, Gamadge."

"No. You haven't met any of the Carringtons?"

"I haven't, but Rose talked about them. Carrington was a very impressive person, elegance personified. He was about sixty-five, I think, this summer. Rose got on with him from the start. I think myself he had remorse about letting his oldest daughter die in want, and was glad to carry out her wishes for Rose. He never knew how badly off the Jenners were, but that was his own fault—he wouldn't communicate after the daughter went off. They met Jenner abroad, and Carrington couldn't bear him. Rose says she wasn't surprised at that, her father wasn't the kind of man Carrington would understand."

"What are the younger Carringtons like?"

"Not so young. Lawrence is or was an art critic, Miss Carrington's a first-class amateur pianist. Rose says they all had a great life together, seeing people and doing things, very happy. But she was too young to enjoy it. She doesn't get much out of *things*—or books either."

"I suppose that you're afraid some kind of case may be built up against her, founded on her lack of alibi?"

"I don't know what kind of case they're building. They might pretend to think anything."

"That she wanted Carrington to finance the marriage, for instance, and that he threatened to cut off supplies now if she didn't drop the idea? It's what he did with his daughter, you say."

"But what good would it do Rose to kill him? She'd get nothing out of that."

"A certain amount of satisfaction, perhaps, if she were an unbalanced person; a paranoiac, say."

"Gamadge, can't you do anything before they—"

"Before they find out that Miss Wakefield's transient and Rose Jenner's love interest are one? Garry, I don't know a thing about paranoia, or schizophrenia, or plain murder for the fun of it. I never in my life could deal with anything but evidence, and there doesn't seem to be much here. If this murder really was the result of an attack of intermittent homicidal mania I won't solve it. But I'm staying, of course."

"You *are*?"

"Over Labor Day anyhow."

"At the Inn? Where? Are you going to let people know you're interested in the case?"

"Not unless it's necessary to tell them. I'm staying at Edgewood."

"At Edgewood?" Yates was astounded.

"My doctor, Hamish," said Gamadge, smiling at him, "who is a very big man indeed, has sent me up to Edgewood because I'm suffering from a slight attack of overwork. Miss Studley is very glad, he informs me, to find

49

that he and I are so sensible. There's a case against Edgewood, you know."

"I should think there was!"

"The patients there are not supposed to be maniacs, intermittent, potential or reformed; but Miss Studley kindly supplied Hamish with the names of their doctors —least she could do—and Hamish, of course, will be able to get details that no layman could ever hope to get. He'll call me up today. He's in town, by the way, on an emergency case, and in a terrible rage about it. But he's rather interested, like everybody else, in the maniac of Frazer's Mills."

Yates had been gazing as if hypnotized at his companion. Now he said: "I always heard you were a hustler, but—"

"Hustler? A couple of telephone calls."

"Gamadge, I don't know what to say."

"Don't say a thing. You go back to the Inn now, and I'll turn up at Edgewood later. We don't know each other if we meet. We'd better *not* meet privately again, but if you feel you must see me call me up as discreetly as you can, and we'll come here."

Yates rose. "I feel as if you could get yourself in anywhere; but I don't know how you're to meet any of the Carringtons, if you want to meet them. I wish to heaven you could meet Rose. But it's a house of mourning."

"Let me worry about that."

"I hoped you might say I was a fool to worry about Rose. Because, even if they did try to make a case against her for Carrington's murder, how could they account for her trying to wipe out the whole village first?"

"You'd be surprised what paranoiacs do for good reasons of their own."

"I thought you didn't know anything about paranoiacs."

"Smattering of general information."

Yates stood looking down at him. At last he said: "Well, I can't tell you how grateful . . ." His voice died. He went to his car, got into it, and bumped across the bridge and down the road. Gamadge watched him go. He finished his cigarette, walked to his car, turned it, and drove back as he had come; all the way back, to the crossroads where the filling station was. There he turned right for Westbury.

6. THE FACTS

Sheriff Ridley got up to shake hands with Gamadge across his desk. "Glad to meet you, Mr. Gamadge. Sit down; have a cigar."

"Thanks very much, Sheriff. I have my cigarettes." Gamadge settled himself in the hard chair indicated, crossed his legs, and tried to look comfortable. He said: "You evidently heard from my friend Durfee."

"I did; glad to make his acquaintance over the telephone." Sheriff Ridley was a stocky, middle-aged man who looked like a small-town storekeeper. He went on, studying Gamadge with some interest: "Told me about some of your cases. I'm glad the two of you took an interest in this one. Well, of course the Carringtons are New York people; naturally New York police are interested."

"Who isn't? It relieves me to find that you don't think I'm butting in too much."

The sheriff rolled a cigar between his fingers, and his eyes were on the green eyes of his guest. He was thinking what that hard-bitten character, Detective Lieutenant Durfee of the New York Police Department (Homicide), had said over the telephone:

"I don't know why he's mixing in up there, Ridley; he probably got interested in something about the case he read in the paper. Don't ask me why he's interested—I wouldn't have said he knew much about homicidal maniacs. Read about 'em, of course, he's read damn near everything. But in your place, if I was stuck the way you are, I'd be glad to have him. . . . No, he isn't in it for publicity; hates being in the papers. If he does find out anything up there he'll dump it right in your lap. If he gets axed himself he'll say he fell downstairs—if he's alive and able to say anything."

The sheriff wanted to know what qualifications Gamadge had.

"Don't ask me," Durfee begged him. "I never found out yet. He'll open a book and find a gun in it. He'll look at a picture and find a letter written in it. He'll study a piece of writing and make out it isn't a laundry list, it's the missing will. I know there's no evidence up there, but he don't like fingerprints.

"He might drive you crazy, he acts so simple. But I wouldn't let that fool me if I was you. Just give him his head and try to forget about him."

The sheriff didn't think that Gamadge acted simple; he seemed on the contrary a businesslike person who mightn't have read a book or looked at a picture in his life. Sheriff Ridley wondered what Durfee could have meant. He said: "Mr. Gamadge, if you can think up anything useful in connection with the case I'll be obliged to you. Moreover, I'm delighted to have another man there —if I could refer to you in that way."

"You can," said Gamadge laughing.

"I wish I had fifteen men to put in that little hell-hole; I've got one deputy there. State police are helping out, but we can't go on like that forever."

"Hell-hole?" Gamadge raised his eyebrows. "I more or less gathered from the papers that Frazer's Mills was a most inoffensive place."

"It is if there was a prowler, and I don't say there wasn't a prowler. He could have cut through the woods to the south-east from Carringtons' and got to the route, east or west of the millpond; thumbed a ride there, or walked home. Matter of twenty minutes if he had a torch, when he certainly did have; plenty of trails through those woods. And these maniacs—their folks take care of them, rather have them kill twenty people in their fits than be shut up where they ought to be."

"But you think it may not have been a prowler after all?"

The sheriff lighted his cigar. When it was drawing properly he went on, more slowly than before:

"This is confidential."

"Of course."

"I wonder if the whole village over there isn't in a conspiracy to cover the feller up."

"You mean they all know somebody's given to seizures, and won't give him away?"

"By village I mean the little houses; all old stock, you know. I don't mean Edgewood or Wakefield's or the Carringtons. I'm not forgetting them, naturally; can't do that. Quite the contrary. Edgewood—the Studley woman swears those doctors don't send up mental cases to her, but people don't go to rest cures because they're well." He looked at Gamadge sideways.

"They certainly don't."

"Wakefield's seems to be out, though that Silver boy only has his family's word for it that he was on his sleeping porch. The Carringtons and that Jenner girl don't seem to have any motive. We'll go back to them later. All I'm saying is that those old-timers in the cottages wouldn't give each other away. I suppose you know something about this Frazer's Mills?"

"I never even heard of it until Friday morning, when it got into the New York papers."

"Peculiar little place. Some bloods settled it a hundred years ago, and built houses for their ex-butlers and grooms and governesses and so forth. The Tavern was run by a retired head groom and his wife; Mrs. Broadbent is the widow of one of their grandchildren." Ridley laughed. "They had to have a tavern, but they never felt the need of a church."

"Godless, were they?"

"Drove in to Westbury, I suppose. It's only five miles around either way. That Miss Bluett that escaped with her life on Thursday night—the librarian—she's descended from one of the original governesses. The point is that

these originals never went away. Stuck there and brought
their husbands and wives back there. It's only in the last
couple of generations that the young people went and
didn't come back. Place is thinning out."

"And really homogeneous," remarked Gamadge.

"That's right, it is. The Tavern quit as a tavern fifty
years ago; Mrs. Broadbent runs the upper part as a boardinghouse—rooming house—but doesn't get roomers often.
Once a year there's a crowd of 'em, when we have our
fair here. Last Thursday night the roomers were all together playing cards, so we let 'em go. Wish we could let
all the other outsiders go, but it isn't possible till after
the inquest on Tuesday.

"There's a general store and post office occupying half
the ground floor of the Tavern, drugstore in the other
half; that's all the business done in Frazer's Mills. Westbury takes care of the village, you know, collects taxes
and mends the road.

"Here's the layout: on the east side of the street we
have all the big houses but one: Carringtons' first as
you drive in, then Wakefield's, then down on the road the
Tavern, then the Rigby Library, then Edgewood. Opposite
are the little houses, ten of 'em; Staplers', where Miss
Bluett boards, and the nine other families or remains of
families. Mostly one or more old people to a house, no
young people except the Stapler boys. Mighty few livings
earned any more, they're all fading out on little pensions
or their savings or what their relations send 'em. Scotch,
English, old American stock. Not a foreigner, not a
stranger.

"Out to the west, way out, are the farms. Same story
—old stock from way back. They don't come to The Mills
much, now that there are no mills; they deal in Westbury."

The sheriff sat back. "Wouldn't you say homicidal
mania might develop in a place like that, or in those
farms?"

"Well," said Gamadge, smiling, "it sounds rather a paradise to me. But I see what you mean."

"I won't go over the list, we've combed the place again and again. They all *act* as if they were afraid of the prowler—I'll say that much. All barricaded up day and night, it's a dead town. I don't know it well myself, they've never had to have any law there before in my time, but they say you wouldn't know it."

Gamadge said that no situation could be more difficult to handle.

"No. And it was the easiest thing in the world for anybody who knew the place at all to make that trip Thursday night. Oh—one more big house, used to be the Compson residence; it's at the end on the west, just about opposite the Carringtons'. A school.

"You understand the whole place is grown up with old trees, and the woods come right down to the back of the properties on the east. Along the edge of the woods, running from behind the Studley place to beyond the Carrington place, there's this walk they call the wood path; just somewheres to take a stroll on a nice day. It's all covered half the time with pine needles and dead leaves, nobody pays to keep it clear now, and you couldn't find a footprint on it to save your life."

"Is that the route the murderer took on Thursday night?"

"We think he must have. He wasn't seen on the street—not that that means much in Frazer's Mills at that hour—and the grounds behind those houses are a network of gardens and grape arbors and waste land. No sign of him there. You can cut up or down from this wood path to the houses, and you can keep to turf all the way." The sheriff took his cigar out of his mouth and looked at it. "I'm not saying a stranger couldn't find it and use it—with a torch.

"This feller, stranger or not, seems to have started at Edgewood, come in by the side door, had a look into old Mrs. Norbury's room at twenty-five past ten. He left and went on to the Library, going up to this wood path, you understand, and along it, and down. He finds the Library door fastened—and wasn't that luck? He goes back up to the wood path and on to the Wakefield Inn. Same thing happens there—a locked door. He leaves the fire axe behind him and goes to Carringtons'."

The sheriff paused, but Gamadge did not interrupt him. He went on:

"It was about ten thirty when he showed up at the Library, about ten forty when Yates got after him at the Inn, about eleven fifteen when the Carringtons locked their front door. The times fit—it doesn't take anywhere near so long to make the trip, detours and all; we've timed it to a possible twenty minutes, going slow, and not counting time out for the Carrington murder. And if he did belong in the Studley place, he had time to get back there—Miss Pepper didn't lock up until half past eleven.

"Our medical examiner got over to Carringtons' with the rest of us half an hour after the Jenner girl found the body; about that, anyway. The Carringtons think she got home and found it around twenty-five after eleven, perhaps a minute or so later. The medical examiner places death not more than an hour earlier, probably not much later than a quarter to eleven."

The sheriff relighted his cigar. Gamadge said: "All very clear."

"Yes. Now let's go back and look at these various stops he made. The first one didn't make any impression on anybody but Mrs. Norbury—in fact nobody heard of it but Miss Pepper, who brushed it off as the old lady's imagination. She's eighty and crippled up with arthritis, which explains why she wasn't more spry about getting out into the hall."

"Where were Miss Studley and Miss Pepper when the prowler came?" asked Gamadge.

"Miss Studley was up on the top floor in her suite, Miss Pepper was in the pantry fixing the old lady's cocoa."

"This side door is to the north, away from the village and protected by trees and shrubbery?"

"Yes. Nothing above Edgewood to the north but road and forest, till you get to the next village—Green Tree."

"And Edgewood—except the top floor—seemed to be in darkness?"

"The ground floor was in darkness, and so was the second-floor hall."

"A visitor might not have noticed, with all the trees and so on, which second-floor rooms were lighted?"

"Probably didn't notice."

"He wandered into a dark hall, up dark stairs into darkness, and tried the first door on the left?"

"That's right."

"As soon as he realized that it was a lighted room, he hurried away?"

"Or just hurried out, if he'd been there all the time."

"Any of them could have gone out and come back and nobody the wiser?"

"Except Mrs. Norbury. She's out on all counts, Miss Pepper was with her after half past ten. So Miss Pepper's out, and Miss Studley answered Miss Wakefield's telephone call at just before eleven."

Gamadge smoked for a few moments in silence. Then he asked: "These patients at Edgewood. What do you think of them?"

"You'll see them; cute idea that, getting yourself into the place. Nothing out of the way about them so far as I could tell, they naturally don't like the idea that they're not free to go. I will say they didn't make as much fuss about it as they might have. Haynes is a New York man, business man, big hardware corporation. Mrs. Turnbull is a widow from Pittsburgh. Motley is staying in New York at the Creighton. I had to laugh—they couldn't say they had to get home on important business, because they're all booked for next week."

"All mentally sound, are they?"

"Miss Studley showed me their doctors' letters. Haynes has a heart condition—his man's a big specialist. Quiet feller, Haynes, widower, good golf player for his age, which is about sixty.

"Motley's thirty-one, up for neuralgia. He looks all right, but I suppose neuralgia don't make spots come out on you, and his doctor wrote that he was in good condition

58

otherwise. No job at present, seems well-fixed and says
he's looking around after doing war work in Washington.

"Mrs. Turnbull's specialist—another big bug—reported
her run down and in need of a change of air. She don't
look up to making that trip Thursday night." The sheriff
fumbled among papers. "Has a right to be run down; husband died in June from accidentally taking too many
sleeping tablets."

"Did he?" Gamadge looked interested.

"I inquired about that, of course, but I understand it
was O.K. The husband was a drinking man, and he took
the stuff with whiskey, regularly every night, last thing before he went to bed. They passed it as an accident in
Pittsburgh. She had the money, by the way, and they say
she was in love with him. Well, that's the Edgewood crowd.
Miss Studley's fighting for 'em—says there isn't a homicidal maniac in the bunch. She's a nice woman, Miss
Studley, you'll like her. So's Miss Pepper. She's married,
has a little boy here in town, lives with his grandmother.
Miss Pepper's husband is a petty officer second class on a
battleship."

"Why didn't she lock up until nearly half past eleven,
when they'd had Miss Wakefield's telephone call half an
hour before?"

"They feel silly about that. Miss Studley came and told
Miss Pepper about the telephone call, and Miss Pepper
told her that they'd already had the visit from the prowler.
They didn't expect him back, so they locked the front
door and stood talking about the situation in the lobby,
and gave him a chance to come back by the side door
and quietly go to bed. Of course it didn't enter their
heads he might belong there with them. Miss Studley still
laughs that idea off; she's just sorry she gave us the loophole."

"And gave him the loophole. Easy-going place, Frazer's
Mills."

"They never had any trouble before. They're not so
easy-going now." The sheriff laughed cynically.

59

"Well, we have the prowler started on his way to the Library. He tried that door, although the Library was lighted."

"That's another reason why I think he was somebody that knew the place. He'd know Miss Bluett was there alone. He wouldn't know who might be in that room at Edgewood—more than one person, perhaps. Miss Bluett wouldn't raise a yell if somebody she knew walked in on her at the Library, no matter how late it was."

"According to the papers, she thought the noise at the door was caused by a squirrel or something; that's why she didn't raise an alarm."

"She's a character. It would take more than a squirrel to scare Hattie Bluett." The sheriff chuckled. "Know why she was working so late?"

"She'd had a consignment of books, hadn't she?"

Ridley went on chuckling. "Typical," he said at last. "She had the consignment because she sent for it—made the Library handy-man take his cart and go and get it at seven o'clock in the evening; made Miss Carrington hustle round and collect the books and send them along, a last lot that wasn't promised until the next week. Right at the time when the family'd be sitting down to their dinner, and a sick man in the house besides! And because why?"

Gamadge shook his head. "Give it up, unless she has delusions of grandeur and likes to make the aristocracy step around."

"There's that too, and it's a kind of a town habit to humor her. But she wanted the books because she intended to take an extra day vacation, and decided to slap the labels in and get the consignment recorded before the weekend. Well, she's still in Frazer's Mills, fit to be tied."

"And not at all impressed by the fact that she barely escaped with her life?"

"Not Hattie Bluett. Well, the prowler went on to the Wakefield Inn, and we know what happened there—at least we know what young Yates says happened, and I don't see why we shouldn't believe him."

"Nor I."

"Miss Homans, both the Silvers, they're accounted for from ten forty-five on; but young Silver—he has a sleeping porch off the parents' room, it's on the south side of the house; the prowler wouldn't see his light. Wouldn't see any light at the Inn."

"You don't feel certain about this Silver boy?"

"Nobody saw him before or afterwards till the police came in after the murder, and the whole town was in the street. Then he showed up, and I questioned him myself. But he couldn't have gone out without the parents knowing it, and they seem like nice people. He's getting ready for college—up here to study. Has a tutor right in Westbury."

"Why a tutor?"

"Didn't pass his examinations or something."

"That sounds as if he hadn't been overworking himself before, whatever he's doing now."

"These adolescents—I don't know. He's a funny feller. You'd better have a look at him."

"Why should he or anybody have left that fire axe behind him, Sheriff, when he went on to the Carringtons'? And if he was already provided with a weapon to use on somebody in Edgewood, or on Miss Bluett, why bother with the fire axe at all?"

"I don't know. I can't even guess, unless he liked the look of the fire axe better than whatever he did have, and then when he heard a young feller call out instead of old Mr. Compson—"

"That's so, a native would expect to find Compson there."

"When he heard Yates call out, perhaps he was panicked and decided he'd better not be caught with the fire axe on him."

"But he didn't use a weapon of his own even at the Carringtons'; did he?"

"He certainly didn't. He used a log of maple wood out of their own parlor fireplace; stood behind a bed curtain and brought it down on the top of Carrington's head, and it crushed the skull as if it had been an iron bar.

Round section of wood, easy enough to handle, that bark don't take prints. And I say he was smart to give up his own weapon and use something that belonged on the premises."

"Carrington was sitting up in bed?"

"Banked up with pillows."

"The murderer must have used both hands."

"Yes, he couldn't hold the bed curtain tight or cover his arms. Plenty of blood, but it washes off some materials and it washes off human skin."

"I suppose some kind of raincoat was worn, Sheriff. It threatened rain that night."

"Yes, and the Jenner girl was wearing a raincoat when she came in, and both the Carringtons have raincoats, and everybody in the place has a raincoat."

"The Carringtons or the Jenner girl could have done it, I gather." Gamadge looked at his cigarette.

"Easy. Carrington says he was back in the library, where he couldn't have seen or heard a thing. Miss Carrington says she was up in her room. The girl needn't have been away from Frazer's Mills at all; the garage is down at the end of the drive south of the house; they usually leave the car and walk up. She can't dig up anybody who saw her in Westbury. But—" the sheriff gnawed his lip.

"Motive missing?"

"Gamadge"—the sheriff leaned forward—"you find me a motive. Just one. The Carringtons and the Jenner girl had nothing to gain and everything to lose by George Carrington's death. He sank his entire capital in an all-out annuity years ago; when he died the income stopped. He had nothing to leave but a couple of thousands in his bank account and the old house—which isn't even wired for electricity—and ten acres of land."

"You looked into his financial situation?"

"I got his lawyer. I got his bank. I got the broker that sold his securities and the agent that sold him the annuity. I saw his papers there at the house. I saw a copy of his will—everything to his son and daughter. He had no life insurance; at least nobody knows anything about it if he had, and nobody's come forward with information. The Carringtons told me all that and I checked everything they said. He wasn't secretive about his affairs.

"You find me a motive for killing George Carrington. And try to connect him up with the others—the near-victims; with old Compson, Bluett, anybody at Edgewood. Or with this Yates. Find out why anybody should want to kill all those people—anybody except a maniac.

"Somebody's crazy, that's all. They say—" he looked at Gamadge almost wistfully—"they say that kind of maniac can fool everybody for years. Is that right?"

"So far as I know."

"And they say we can only hope to prevent the last of a series of crimes. Not the next one, oh no. If the feller was crazy enough to run the risks he ran on Thursday night he'll be crazy enough to run more. And he still has his own weapon, whatever it may be."

Gamadge rose, and the sheriff wondered again what Durfee meant by implying that this matter-of-fact and down-to-earth character was some kind of curiosity. Nice enough man, seemed intelligent, but not what the sheriff's wife would call colorful.

"It's a tough case," said the colorless one. "When is the inquest?"

"It's been adjourned to Tuesday, and after that how can I keep all these people here? I can't." Ridley sat looking up at Gamadge, holding his dead cigar. "The Edgewood people are backed by their doctors. The Silvers are getting a lawyer."

"How are the Carringtons taking it all?"

"They're behaving like decent sensible people. The girl's been sick in bed since she found the body."

Gamadge said: "I can't get into that house, Sheriff, unless we take Lawrence Carrington into our confidence."

"You mean tell him why you're here?"

"We'll have to tell him. I wonder if you'd ring him up?

63

You might say I'm investigating Edgewood—it happens to be true." Gamadge pondered. "You could tell Carrington I need local information. And don't I!"

"You certainly ought to get into the Carrington house."

"And meet the Carringtons and Miss Jenner. I couldn't manage it without you."

"I'll ring him," said the sheriff slowly. He got up and put out a hand. "Glad to have met you."

"Don't make it so final, Sheriff," said Gamadge, smiling. "We might meet again, you know."

"Let's hope we do."

7. DESCENDANTS

Gamadge drove into Frazer's Mills at noon. He stopped his car at the entrance to the village and sat looking down the long, broad, shady street. A month later these oaks and maples, planted here a century before, would be on fire with every shade of red and yellow; so would the forests to the right. On the left fields rolled away to a distant farm or two, white against dark-green hills.

"Emptied of its folk, this pious morn." Gamadge wondered sardonically whether any soul *could* return to tell why The Mills was desolate. Not if the soul were already there.

Desolate it seemed, with more than a Sunday quiet; not a living creature in sight, not even a—Gamadge bethought himself: No dogs in Frazer's Mills? Or didn't they bark at night? Or were they all shut up in the houses after dark? Or had the prowler's muffled feet made no noise at all?

Here was a living creature at last, but one who only gave sinister significance to the empty scene. A young state police officer wheeled his motorcycle into view from a driveway on the right and stood it beside a mounting block.

Gamadge leaned out and waved at him. He came to the car window; a thickset young man, sandy and fresh-faced.

"My name's Gamadge. Did you"—Gamadge was fumbling for his wallet—"get any word?"

"Yes, sir. My name's Adey." He glanced at Gamadge's

65

license and returned it. "Other man's Vines. I'll see him if you don't, he might be along the Green Tree Road."

"One at each end?"

"Yes."

"Well, you'll be right on hand if there's another murder."

The young man, startled, answered sharply: "Why would there be?"

"These things are supposed to run in a series, aren't they?"

"Yes, but he got away."

"But you expect him back?"

Officer Adey said shortly: "We can't be sure it was somebody from outside."

"But you don't think so. Excuse me for asking these questions, it's what I'm here for, as you know."

Adey nodded. "I know the place too well. My aunt lives in one of those." He inclined his head forward and to the right.

"One of the cottages? You don't tell me. You're a descendant?"

"Yes, but he was a trainer."

"That's something!"

"Compsons' stables. His bay geldings won every trotting race at Westbury for twenty-five years."

"Good for him!"

Officer Adey accepted a cigarette and a light. He leaned an elbow on the car door and looked along the street with an air of challenge. "I helped them with the checkup Thursday night. You should have seen the place."

"Turmoil?"

"I couldn't tell you what it looked like. There's only two street lamps, most of it's dark. The whole town was out after we got here and they heard our motors and the cars from Westbury. There was an old lady from Edgewood in a Mother Hubbard with flowers; there was somebody from Wakefield's been shampooing her hair, tied up in a wet towel. There was nightgowns and pajamas. There was Miss Wakefield's transient in a bathrobe, and Law-

66

rence Carrington in a soup and fish. I tell you it was a pitcher."

"You make me see it. You checked up, did you?"

"All the cottages. Every able-bodied person has an alibi—like the salesmen at the Tavern. With their families or visiting around or at the store. Nobody's bothering about the cottages, and I understand Edgewood has no maniacs. There's that Silver boy, funny feller, but his folks didn't act to me as if they were concealing anything. Carringtons—they don't come up here as much as they used to, but unless they've changed a good deal they're a family with no bats at all. Nice people. The old man came across with a big present for our dance at Christmas —came across regular. That girl they have there—she don't drive as if she was crazy, anyhow."

"I see you're sold on the prowler. Your opinion's valuable, officer. How about dogs?"

"Dogs? Oh, you mean Thursday night. That don't mean anything. There's no dogs at Edgewood or Wakefield's or Carringtons', and of course none at the Library, and there's always a little barking going on of an evening, the usual thing. If you know the lay of the land you can understand that the prowler wouldn't get near enough to any of the cottages to start any real barking." He mused sadly: "Miss Wakefield always had a lot of nice bird dogs, but they've died off and she says she can't feed 'em good any more; so she's quit worrying."

"I should think she'd have enough to do to feed the boarders. Well, thanks very much. I'll be going along."

Gamadge drove slowly along the street. He passed the rambling old Compson house on the left, shut up tight for the duration of the school holidays; on his right, barely discernible behind its maples, rose the classic façade of Carringtons'; Gamadge had a glimpse of a side lawn with round flowerbeds, and a pointed towerlike trellis half hidden by vines. The front lawn, green and cool under its thick trees as the bottom of the sea, was separated from the narrow flagged footway by a white picket fence and a hedge.

More trees, and then the Wakefield house; of red brick, handsome and stately, with modern additions that were no doubt a necessity. Gamadge noted the large screened sleeping porch where the Silver boy had or had not been on Thursday night at the time of the murder, and looked back after passing to get a view of the famous side door.

The Tavern, with its low pillared frontage and its wide old doorways, pleased Gamadge's eye; but one window was full of hardware, the other of cosmetics and toothpaste. The drugstore was open for business, but nobody stood at the soda fountain.

Far back among its evergreens, enclosed by a thick and tall privet hedge, the smallish Library presented high casement windows to the street. Its front faced north, and could not be seen at all behind the greenery. A charming little old house, the Rigby house, of gray brick freshly painted. Gamadge wondered whether there might not be interesting old reading matter on its shelves.

Edgewood was trim and well-kept, with extensive grounds. Gamadge looked past it to the wilder spaces behind, which seemed to merge with the woods themselves; but the fatal little path must be there. The house was square and plain with a south wing, painted white. It had blue shutters, which gave it a modern look. Gamadge turned up the neat driveway, and got out in front of a small porch. The front door was closed, and—as Gamadge discovered—locked. He rang.

A pleasant girl in white, with a cap, evidently Miss Pepper, opened the door a crack and peeped out. Then she opened the door wide.

"You must be Mr. Gamadge," she said, smiling at him.

"I am."

"We're expecting you. The man will take care of your car and your bags."

"Only one bag."

"Didn't you bring golf clubs?" Miss Pepper looked past him at the car.

"No, the doctor says golf makes me nervous."

"It certainly upsets some of our guests. Come in, Miss

68

Studley's downstairs. We hoped you'd get here in time for lunch."

The big lounge had a stairway rising from it to the left, a generous fireplace, now banked with autumn flowers, comfortable deep chairs and sofas, plenty of tables for magazines and ash trays. There was a window on either side of the front door, one in the left wall, one in the right, and two at the rear.

Miss Pepper went through an archway on the right, and presently another white-uniformed figure appeared in her place.

"Mr. Gamadge?"

As Gamadge shook hands with Miss Studley he understood why Edgewood had been a success. She looked firm and competent enough to deal with the prowler himself, and yet she looked indulgent.

"I don't have any office down here," she explained. "I try to keep away from anything institutional."

Gamadge said he never intended to become an inmate of an institution while he had the use of his arms and legs.

"I know, that's how everybody feels. I'll take you up to the third floor and show you my office—anybody can go in or out of it night or day. In fact they do!" she laughed. "I keep some good interesting books up there, and I also keep nice sharp pencils and pads and things. Everybody wants pencils all the time."

"Doesn't it disturb you frightfully?"

"Oh no, I have my bedroom. I don't even hear people when they walk into the office and shove things around. Nobody knocks at my bedroom door except in great emergency—it's an unwritten law."

"I'm glad you have one at least."

Miss Studley thought this was as cool and poised a customer, for an allegedly nervous one, as she had ever seen. But these writers, you never could tell. Or had Dr. Hamish said that Gamadge was a writer? He didn't look quite like a writer. She had had a writer or two—most of them couldn't afford Edgewood, of course. Those she had had—Miss Studley winced mentally. She asked: "Are you a writer, Mr. Gamadge?"

"Now and then. Nothing to boast about. I'm supposed to examine old books and papers."

Miss Studley accepted this because she had to. There was something about this Mr. Gamadge that took the eye, and she didn't know what it was. A nice man anyway, and a cool one.

"I had a very nice telephone conversation with your doctor," she said. "I was delighted to have the chance to get acquainted with Dr. Hamish."

"You must have talked to most of the top men in that profession, Miss Studley."

"I've talked to a lot of them. And they've never let me down." Miss Studley looked at him calmly. "I'm glad ~ou're both so sensible about poor little Frazer's Mills. This panic is absurd."

"Er—a certain amount of alarm was natural at first."

"At first, yes; though it was perfectly obvious the lunatic went away after the murder. Do sit down."

Gamadge waited until she had taken a chair, and then sat in another near her, beside a table. Miss Studley pushed an ash tray towards him and he got out his cigarettes. She shook her head when he offered one.

"I smoke now and then to be sociable, that's all."

"Better for me if I could say the same. You mean you think that after the Carrington murder the fellow, having had what he came for, just kept going?"

Miss Studley thought this over. Then she said: "Yes, going south; through the woods to the Westbury road. As for his being still in the woods, that's silly; they've hunted everywhere."

Gamadge, looking through the nearest back window, said that there seemed to be a lot of woods.

"Miles of them, but they've been searched. All the game wardens, and they know every foot of the woods, and the state police, and a posse from Westbury. It's a shame that The Mills should be avoided as if it had an epidemic in it."

"It did look a trifle abandoned as I came through. I thought the inhabitants themselves must—"

"They have this foolish idea that some of our guests from outside—some one of them, I mean, of course—might have had an attack of some sort. As if there wouldn't be premonitory symptoms!"

"There certainly ought to be. Are you a native of The Mills, Miss Studley?"

"I was born right in that fourth cottage, the one with the latticed porch and the dahlias."

"No! A descendant!"

"I certainly am," said Miss Studley, smiling, "and I'll tell you something else. My great-grandmother was a nurse in the Chapley family, and where do you think the Chapleys lived?"

"Right here?" Gamadge smiled back at her.

"Right in this house!"

"Well, you've managed to do something or other to the wheel of destiny, Miss Studley."

"It does seem like fate. I always loved this Chapley house, and as soon as I could I bought it." She looked around her with pride. "It wasn't well arranged inside, those old country homes were apt to be so cut up and dark; so I tore out every partition downstairs, and just kept this one room, and the dining room in the wing. I built a new kitchen and laundry on."

"What a good idea."

"And I put private baths in upstairs."

"You had vision."

"I've certainly done very well."

"Did this prowler thing scare any of your patients away?"

Miss Studley's face fell. "It's too silly—they're not allowed to go."

"Why not?"

"That's what I'd like to have somebody tell me. Mrs. Norbury is the only witness—you know he nearly went into her room?"

"Yes, I remember."

"You'd think, being eighty years old, she'd be prostrated, crying and begging to go home. She's reveling in it!"

Gamadge laughed. "Likes the excitement?"

"Really it's quite ghoulish. After all, Mr. Carrington was killed! But I don't know, sometimes very old people seem to lose all sense of tragedy."

"So near the edge themselves that it doesn't shock them when somebody else goes over?"

"I can't help thinking so. She wouldn't leave for anything—she's quite looking forward to the inquest. But poor Mrs. Turnbull—so nervous and frightened, and won't take sedatives because her husband—I'm not betraying confidences, it was all in the papers at the time."

"What happened to him?"

"He took an overdose of amytal. I do wish people wouldn't run these risks. He had definite instructions from his doctor. But no, he must take twenty grains instead of five, and of course he was found dead in the morning. Poor Mrs. Turnbull, and now this happens. You can imagine how she must feel, practically suspected of being a homicidal maniac."

"She has plenty of company, though."

"Mr. Haynes—the quietest, nicest man; he doesn't say much, but it can't be good for his heart. And Mr. Motley—cooped up like this and not even able to go somewhere in his car and play golf! I'm sure their lawyers could get them out of it, but they don't want to fuss. If they did, somebody would be sure to say they were running off."

"But they'd have to come back for the inquest if they're to give evidence."

"They have no evidence to give. They don't know any more about it than I do. I may be very wrong about it, but I do wish Mrs. Norbury hadn't said a word about her door opening on Thursday night; then we wouldn't be in it. But the minute the news of the murder came she was out in the street talking to the police and the sheriff and the newspapers. If it wasn't for Mrs. Norbury

nobody would ever have thought of saying that one of
the Edgewood guests started out from here on Thursday
night. What with? That's what I'd like to know. We
haven't missed any axes." Miss Studley glanced at Gamadge and away. "Of course it's made the others nervous,"
she said. "But as I told Dr. Hamish, and he understood
perfectly and sent you up, all the doctors swear these people weren't mental at all. You don't develop a thing like
that in a couple of days, you know."

Gamadge said: "If the prowler was from outside, and
came in along the Green Tree road, this would be the
first house on his way."

"Of course it would, and so I tell everybody. Mr.
Gamadge . . ."

"Yes, Miss Studley?"

"They all lock their doors at night now, and it wouldn't
be fair for me not to tell you to lock yours."

"Good for you. That's the way to talk."

"Well, after all, I'm responsible for the safety of my
guests. Outsiders—the newspapers—keep talking about our
leaving the house open so late. Imagine. Everybody here
always left their houses open as late as they liked, sometimes all night. And as for our not locking the side door
on Thursday after Miss Wakefield called up—"

"Didn't you?"

"Mr. Gamadge, just please put yourself in our place.
Nothing ever happened in The Mills. Now this prowler
came, looked in on Mrs. Norbury and went away again,
looked in at the Inn and went away again, evidently
going south. There hadn't been any murder so far as we
knew. Why in the world should we think he'd come back,
anyway? We locked the front door, it was about the time
Miss Pepper did lock it. But we didn't lock the back
doors; normally we left the kitchen door until the staff
came home. They like to stay around in Westbury for a
while after the late movies, having sodas or beer or whatever they do have."

Gamadge said: "I see your point. You weren't in a
panic."

"And we didn't want Mrs. Norbury getting into one, either. We weren't going to tell her about the Wakefield business at all. Well, I know one thing; even if they don't find this prowler, it won't take long for The Mills to keep their doors unlocked again."

Gamadge laughed. "No, it never takes long."

"And that's one good thing." Miss Studley took a booklet out of her pocket. "You'd better look at our rates. I thought you might like this nice south room on the second floor, with bath."

Gamadge looked at the price of the south room, repressed a shudder, and said it would be fine. "I may not be staying after Labor Day, you know, Miss Studley. Depends on what goes on at home."

Miss Studley rose. "I hope you can stay longer. You're just what we need, Mr. Gamadge—somebody sensible."

"Well," said Gamadge, also getting to his feet, "of course I wasn't here at the time."

"I suppose that makes a difference."

They went up the curving stairs, Miss Studley explaining that there was a telephone booth behind them, to the right of the side door. When they reached the second story landing she nodded towards the left. "There's that side staircase, and that's Mrs. Norbury's room just this side of it. My office is just above. Shall we go up and look at it? So you'll know where to come when you want a pencil or a novel or a piece of writing paper."

"I have a pencil and a novel and a piece of writing paper, but I'd feel much safer if I knew how to track you to your lair."

"My lair is my bedroom," laughed Miss Studley.

"Oh yes, I forgot."

They went down the hall and climbed the side stairs. On the top floor Miss Studley opened the first door to the left. Gamadge looked into a large plastered room with a sloping ceiling and a dormer window. It was simply a comfortable sitting room with a large, well appointed desk.

"Awfully nice," said Gamadge, "but where do you keep the secret files?"

"I have none, of course!"

"No case histories?"

"They're not my business. And any records I do make for the doctors—"

"They're in your bedroom. I know."

"What of it?"

"I'm beginning to think this is the best run sanatorium I ever saw or heard of."

"It isn't a sanatorium." Miss Studley couldn't help laughing with him. "Are you making me out some kind of fraud?"

"Tell me who isn't one, when dealing with the sick?"

"They're not sick any more than you are, and if you're sick, then I am!"

"Can't a man be tired examining books and documents?"

"I should think he'd die of it."

They went down and along the second floor hall to the south room, where Gamadge found his bag. He said it was as pleasant a room as he had ever seen. "All blue and white—so cheerful." He didn't like blue and white, but the south room was certainly cheerful.

"Come down when you're ready," said Miss Studley, "lunch is from one to two. The dining room is through that arch from the lounge, and there's a big screened porch off it where we serve tea. It's glassed for a sun parlor in wintertime."

Gamadge, left to himself, looked out of his south window. He could see little of the Library, there were too many trees. He unpacked his bag, got ready for lunch, and went downstairs; but he went by way of the side stairs, and stood for a while looking out of the side door. Then he turned back past the telephone closet and went through the lounge into the dining room.

8. CASE HISTORIES

Although it was only one o'clock, Gamadge found four little tables already occupied. The four guests looked up at him as he arrived, then down at their plates again. He glanced at them, unfolding his napkin.

The older man, sandy and graying, must be Haynes; he looked depressed and gloomy, and he took small interest in the newcomer. Ancient Mrs. Norbury, alert as a sparrow, seemed to accept Gamadge as a refreshing novelty in a stale situation. She smiled at him.

Gamadge returned the smile; they bowed.

His eye caught the flash of sunlight on Mrs. Turnbull's bracelet, and he raised his eyes from it to her face. The nervous widow; she had had the money, and she had loved Mr. Turnbull. Had he perhaps chosen to cease upon the midnight? Gamadge thought that he himself might have done so in Mr. Turnbull's place. A dull woman, and (unless Gamadge was mistaken) without benevolence.

The dark fellow in the corner—Motley—showed more inner discomfort than the rest of them. In fact, he showed agitation. His handsome mouth twitched as if he had recurrent twinges of his neuralgia, his eyes roved, his hands —well manicured—played with the silver, and he dropped a spoon to the floor. The rosy-faced waitress picked it up for him, and he smiled upon her.

All I know about them, thought Gamadge, is that three of them are nervous and have a right to be, and that all four of them must be rich. Motley's very nervous. Just bored? If I were mixed up in a murder and for some reason didn't care for publicity, how *damned* nervous I should be.

Gamadge hurried through his excellent lunch to get to the lounge first. Mrs. Norbury came out next, and paused beside his chair. He rose.

"I'm Mrs. Norbury," she said brightly.

"My name's Gamadge."

"Oh, we all know who you are. Came right along into the midst of the maniacs, didn't you?" She chuckled. "How do you like us?"

"Very much. But you were one of the near victims, Mrs. Norbury."

"Yes, and they're all wild at me because I told about it, and got them all caged up under suspicion. But wouldn't you have told in my place?"

"Certainly. Very wrong of you not to have said anything."

"They ought to be much obliged to you, anyway; takes the blight off."

"I must admit that I didn't know there was going to be such a blight; I mean so much effect of curfew and martial law in the village."

"It's too bad they don't catch this tramp. These police!"

"But it needn't be a tramp, Mrs. Norbury."

"No, that's the trouble. I do hope since you've come there'll be a chance of bridge tonight."

"Won't they play?"

"Never touch a card. Say they couldn't keep their minds on it. Oh well, perhaps you'll feel like rummy."

"I do hate that game so."

"I do too, but it's better than nothing." She went up the stairs. Haynes, Motley and Mrs. Turnbull came in from the dining room together; companies in misfortune, if in nothing else but bridge. Haynes said: "You're Mr. Gamadge."

"Yes."

"I'm Haynes, let me introduce you to Mrs. Turnbull. This is Motley."

They all nodded. Mrs. Turnbull stood twisting her pearls

with ringed fingers and looking at Gamadge a little vacantly. Motley went to the back of the room and stared out of a window; Haynes turned abruptly to fling open the front door. He gazed out into the brightness of the afternoon.

"Stuff and nonsense," he growled. "Broad daylight, and a policeman at each end of the village, and a deputy sheriff on the Carringtons' front steps; and we're all shut up like dangerous animals."

Mrs. Turnbull spoke in a mincing voice; "But after all, Mr. Haynes—a crazy man with a stick of wood might rush in before anybody could stop him. Do you think it's quite safe to open the door?"

"Fellow's in the next state by this time. We'll hear of some crime in Jersey. Plenty of woods there!"

Motley spoke with his back to them:

"If that Norbury woman had kept her mouth shut . . . I still think it may have been a coincidence. I told that idiot sheriff so. I told the captain of state police so."

Gamadge, interested, repeated: "Coincidence?"

Motley swung to face him. "That incident here on Thursday night. Place like this—people are popping in and out of rooms all the time. It's understaffed. We're paying for a lot of service we don't get. Pepper's always in a hurry, and the maids are always forgetting clean towels or something. Somebody opened and shut Mrs. Norbury's door and won't admit it now, somebody went out for a breath of air—it was stifling that night—and doesn't dare say so because if they do they'll be thrown into jail as a criminal lunatic. Mrs. Norbury's eighty. She got things mixed, and when the murder broke she had hindsight and made her story fit the other stories."

"Well, of course," said Gamadge, "it does fit the other stories."

"She told Pepper at the time," added Haynes. "No use trying that kind of thing, Motley, it won't help."

Mrs. Turnbull said: "The best thing to do is just to wait quietly until it blows over." Her voice quavered. "They can't keep us forever."

She went over to the stairs and mounted them laboriously; lamed by her high heels. Not a woman, Gamadge thought, who had ever had much physical exercise. Well on in her forties.

Motley stood looking after her, an ugly look. Haynes caught it.

"I don't put it on her," he said. "She's neurasthenic, I suppose, bound to be after the shock she had when her husband died like that. But I'd say she was incapable of it in more ways than one."

Motley cast an angry glance at him. "I don't put it on her. Never thought of such a thing. It's this passive acceptance of the thing that gets me. She has nothing to do but sit here and wait forever. The rest of us can't."

"By heaven," said Haynes, "I'm glad the lunatic didn't try *her* door. She'd have gone off her head."

"Good thing if she had. Settled it then and there—he'd have been caught."

"Nice thing for us if he never is caught!"

Gamadge said: "I suppose he must have had a torch with him on that trip of his."

"That doesn't worry them." Haynes turned a pale blue eye towards him. "There's a torch here, in a coat closet off the side lobby. Anybody can use it. Everybody does. Dark as pitch out there at the back until you get through to the garage."

"And does everybody use that wood path?"

"If they want a walk. It's an easy enough way to get one, and trails lead off it into the woods."

"And we all have raincoats," said Motley with a sardonic half-smile. "And there's always plenty of grass and pine needles sticking to our shoes—even Mrs. Turnbull's. That man of Miss Studley's cleans them when he feels like it."

"I'm sure I don't know what's worrying you people," said Gamadge, "with so little evidence, and what there is distributed around like that."

Haynes gave him a lowering look. "You don't? How about going home again, and our friends waiting to see whether we'll take a swing at them with a piece of wood?"

"They won't. Too many people in the boat with you."

Motley came to the foot of the stairs. He said: "They might look into those cottages again."

"Thought they were all alibied."

"By one another. This is an inbred, backwards community, nobody in it had the spunk to leave—they've sat here for a hundred years drying out. As for those farms—"

Miss Pepper came through from the archway, to answer the telephone which had begun to ring behind the stairs. She returned and smiled at Gamadge: "Your doctor's checking up on you."

"Is he? Good. This the only telephone, Miss Pepper?" asked Gamadge, starting for it.

"Miss Studley has one in her office on the top floor."

Gamadge stopped. "Oh—by the way; where *is* Miss Studley? I wanted a word with her if she isn't busy."

"Out on the porch."

"Thanks. I'll see her."

Gamadge went back and around to the left; he paused a moment to glance at the lobby, the side door and the side stairs; then he entered the booth and shut the door.

"Hamish?"

"Hello, idiot. How's audibility?"

"I looked into that. Safe here, you don't have to worry about anybody but the operator in Westbury; and Westbury's a good-sized place."

"Bother all this top-secret stuff of yours."

"You never have any of course."

"Mine doesn't spring from morbid curiosity. Well, I got the information for you."

"You're a wonder."

"A nice job it was."

"For Miss What's-her-name, your poor unfortunate secretary. All in the interests of public welfare, too, and no curiosity, morbid or healthy. Well, I'm greatly obliged all the same."

"You should be. Number one in order of age: the old party is perfectly regular. His man—I know him—

says he had his tonsils out and gets sore throat at sea level and can't stand mountains on account of his heart. This Edgewood is just right for him. His specialist often sends such cases there. Known him for thirty years, and damn it all it's impossible—any such development as you're interested in."

"That satisfies me."

"The next party, the one from Pittsburgh—I had the dickens of a time running her man down. He's very well-known. By the way, who's paying these long distance calls? I have a carefully itemized list."

"Blow you to dinner."

"See that you do. I suppose you know this party's interesting history? Husband died in June from an over-dose of his own amytal. Took twenty grains in whiskey one night. She was knocked out. He was the family chauffeur."

"Was he?"

"Love match on her part. Her father seems to have been a queer old tyrant, one of the original steel magnates. After her mother died he told her he'd leave her every cent he had if she'd stay and take care of him. So as soon as he died she married this fellow, the only man she ever saw. He started in drinking, but otherwise turned out satisfactory to her."

"Why didn't she know other men?"

"They weren't quite in society, father too much of a rough diamond, and the specialists—he took care of them both—says she's not particularly bright or attractive. So the papers didn't play the tragedy up as much as they might if the circumstances had been more interesting. Of course it got lots of publicity in Pittsburgh."

"Where did the tragedy occur?"

"Right there in the family mansion; house party on. But the specialist says there isn't a thing the matter with her but too much time on her hands and losing her Clarence, no insanity in the family, she's never depressed. He'd go to court on it, she hasn't the makings of schizo-phrenia. Or anything else that makes you kill total strangers. Like the other party, she'd never even heard of the place—Edgewood. He found it for her from some other doctor."

"Thanks, that'll do quite well."

"Now we come to the junior member of the triumvirate, and he did suggest coming to Edgewood—thought of it himself."

"Really?"

"I never got hold of his man at all, he's on a fishing trip; but he has an office with three other G.P.s in a big mid-town professional building, and I got hold of the head office nurse yesterday. She knows all about it, every detail.

"This building is handy to a lot of the big hotels, and they get a lot of practice from out-of-town people. Our party called up from the Creighton last week and said he didn't know a doctor in town, he was on from Washington; he had this hellish neuralgia. Could the receptionist in the building recommend a physician? The receptionist often does. She got him connected with this G.P., who's a first-rate man and has a big practice. He made an appointment for our party. The party came around. Has definite eye trouble, which our man spotted; it kept him out of the war. Might easily mean neuralgia now and then. Not another thing the matter with him, they gave him the works as usual; seemed perfectly all right except for this attack of neuralgia, which of course you can't spot for yourself. However, it's a nasty thing.

"Well, you know what we do when there's nothing to be done."

"I know. You send us somewhere else."

"Nothing like change of air and scene; and Mr. Motley had his place all picked out. He'd heard this Edgewood was just what he needed. So nurse gets Edgewood on the telephone, and Miss Studley talks to the doctor, and it's all fixed. He could tell her the party wasn't alcoholic, mental or developing mumps, and it was pretty obvious from his hotel and the way he looked that he could pay the bill. He offered to pay the doctor's in cash, by the way, seeing he was a stranger, and the offer was accepted with many thanks. But he was at the Creighton, all right; the doctor called him there to tell him that Edgewood could take him."

"Hamish, you're a most competent man."

"No! You really think so? How can I express—"

"The office nurse seems to think that we can wash our friend out as a mental hazard?"

"Absolutely, but of course they haven't his history, except what he gave them, and there has to be a first time. But the nurse says she never saw anybody less likely to fill that bill. And there was no war experience to create any kind of neurosis, you remember; unless you could get it in Washington. Well, I'll wait for your report with interest. Anything so far?"

"Not much. Just got to the place. I suppose these doctors won't stir anything up on the strength of your inquiries?"

"Oh Lord, the last thing they want is a fuss. They're always afraid of any talk about carelessness in diagnosis. As if even a psychiatrist could be certain—"

"I know. Thanks. Hamish, that dinner will be something to remember."

Gamadge hung up. He consulted a notebook and called a number.

"Well, well," said Detective-Lieutenant Durfee, Homicide: "How's things so far?"

"All right. I wish you'd be kind enough to get me some information, Durfee."

"I wish you'd give me some; I still don't know why you were so bound to go up there and look for a maniac."

"Just interested. It's such a queer case."

"Isn't it? Was it a prowler?"

"So they tell me. Durfee, I want to know something, and I wouldn't ask a newspaper for anything. I don't want these people hounded unnecessarily. I thought the Pittsburgh police would keep quiet if you asked them to."

"The who?"

"The Pittsburgh police."

Durfee said after a pause, "You mean that woman there at Edgewood."

"You know how I am, Durfee, I always want to know all about everything. There may be nothing to it. I simply thought you might get me all the details on the quiet—about that accidental death in June."

"It was in the papers."

"But I didn't pay any attention at the time, and the police there would have a lot of details the papers never had—if they're any good at all."

"What details?" Durfee added after another pause: "No motive; I looked it up myself when this thing broke. They put her in the clear. She had all the money, and he wasn't running around with anybody. He was too smart for that."

"I know. I want details about the people who were in the house at the time, and a full description."

"What *is* this?"

"Nothing, probably, and it would be most unfair to make more trouble for the woman just to satisfy my curiosity."

"They'll keep quiet if I ask them to—I could explain that I want all the angles. The case is closed, you know."

"Let it stay that way. It probably will."

"I never knew anybody poked around the way you do; and I never knew you to do it before without being invited to. What's the connection between an overdose of amytal, no matter how administered, and somebody going around killing everybody with a log of wood?"

"None whatever, I imagine."

"And I suppose you want this information right away?"

"The sooner the better. Get it out of the picture."

Durfee muttered something and hung up. Gamadge hung up also, and with his hands in his pockets sauntered across the lounge and out on the porch. Haynes stood against the rail, smoking.

A tall, slender man in tweeds came along the street; he was hatless, and his blond head was bent. Without looking up, he turned into the Edgewood drive.

"Good Lord," said Haynes, "that's Carrington."

9. INSIDE STUFF

Carrington raised his head, and Gamadge said rather loudly: "I know him."

Haynes stared.

"Never entered my thick head that it was the Carrington I knew in town." Gamadge started down the steps. Carrington, taking his cue, raised an arm in salutation. They met and shook hands.

"Mr. Gamadge." Carrington spoke low.

"Yes. I hope this means that you approve of my idea, Mr. Carrington."

"Approve? I can't tell you how relieved I was when Ridley called up before lunch. He says the New York people think you can really do something—if anybody can."

"Don't count on it. We'd better make ourselves solid with Haynes."

"I imagine so."

They walked side by side up the walk to the steps. Haynes was still staring, but as they arrived he turned his head and scattered cigarette ash among the shrubs below the railing.

Carrington said: "This is Mr. Haynes, I think."

Haynes met his eyes. "Yes, I'm Haynes." He cleared his throat.

"I saw you at Westbury Town Hall on Friday. I'm very glad, Mr. Haynes, to have this opportunity to express my regret that you and Miss Studley's other guests should be put to this wretched inconvenience. I wish you'd tell them so."

Haynes, his blue eyes fixed upon Carrington in embarrassment, muttered something to the effect that it was kind of Carrington to think of other people just now.

"Like to express my sympathy," he said.

"Thank you. I suppose the authorities have their routine, but really I do think it unnecessary in this case. All I can say is that I'm sorry."

Haynes cleared his throat again. "I assure you these people—it's unthinkable."

"I agree."

"Well—glad to have seen you." He turned and walked into the house, closing the door after him. Carrington watched him go. When the door was shut he said wearily: "Poor devil. It is a shame. And the woman—what's her name?—Turnbull. And the other fellow. Fellow victims in the Carrington tragedy." He looked about him. "We might sit down on the steps for a minute. Or—" he glanced upwards to right and left.

Gamadge said: "It's all right—nobody in those rooms. I took the liberty of looking into them as I came down to lunch."

Carrington smiled faintly: "Part of the system?"

"Part of the system."

They sat down on an upper step, and Carrington got out his pipe. While he filled and lighted it, Gamadge considered him.

The terrible experience which he had undergone must have left its mark on him, but Gamadge wondered whether he was much changed by it outwardly; he was so obviously a man of great emotional reserve, the type of man who makes a virtue of facing the world with self-possession. He might not even be a man of deep feeling; but he was sensitive. His control was probably the result of long years of training.

His eyes, deep-set and far apart, were slightly reddened, perhaps by the strain of these last bad nights; his nostrils looked pinched, his mouth was pressed into a close line, a deep groove scored it on either side from nose to chin. A sensitive face, forced into the semblance of a mask by an effort of will.

Gamadge wondered whether profit of any kind, financial or other, could induce or drive a man of Carrington's type to murder, much less parricide. He thought that such a man would not even be tempted to violence by considerations of gain. And in this case the loss of money had occurred years before; Carrington had not had more to lose than a country-house, its contents and its surrounding acres; there was no evidence that he had been in danger of losing even them. Unthinkable that he would have committed such a crime for them, no matter what his sentimental feeling for the place. Unthinkable, even if by their loss he had been threatened with beggary; and he had never been threatened with beggary.

Carrington, his pipe going, now considered Gamadge in his turn. He took the pipe out of his mouth, smiled, and said: "Ridley made it plain that you're a remarkable person, Mr. Gamadge. But I confess I can't quite see why —or how—a man of your kind ever took up this sort of work. Not that it isn't in the highest degree useful work; and I ought to have heard of you before. But my tastes are narrow and my experience limited."

"Much better not to spread yourself out as thin as some of the rest of us do. As for my interest in criminology—my applied interest in it —I sometimes feel inclined to ask people who express surprise at it how I could have avoided it."

"You mean your own profession ran along parallel lines?"

"Very much so. The alleged crime," said Gamadge, smiling, "the clues, the proof (if I'm lucky), and the pursuit and punishment of the criminal."

"You stick to the good old formula of crime and punishment?"

"Oh, yes; I stick to that. And to me, you know, there's something almost murderous in the forgery of a book or a letter. Something's murdered if the thing comes off; reality, confidence, and—er—integrity."

you won't see an open doorway or a soul on the walks.
Perhaps you'd *better* drive. I don't know. They say they've
searched the woods, but I'd back a boy scout to hide up
and not be found. Caves, rocks"—he glanced ·to the
left—"trees. Why not hide in a tree? One reads of such
cases—madmen living for weeks and months in the woods,
living on God knows what. Perhaps you'd better drive."

"I will."

"You don't laugh, I'm glad to see."

"No, I don't laugh."

"As for a madman in the cottages or farms—that's out
of the question. I know these people, I know them all. As
you see, the landowners kept their tenantry"—he smiled
—"under their eye. People think that's very odd—that
the cottages should have been put in full view of the big
houses; but people don't get the idea, which is quite sensible—the village at the gates of the Manor. And the cottages are very nice. You can't see much of them, never
could, behind their trees. I only wish the Tavern were
fulfilling its ancient functions, but local option was too
much for us, and there'd be no business nowadays. Not
enough custom to keep a bar going. Well, my sister and
I will never desert, and Emeline Wakefield won't. After
that . . . Fact is, the little place is dying. After our day
it will turn into something else—artists' colony or weekend resort for New York people."

"If I had your place I think I could live and die in it."

"Not a bad place to die. The cemetery's along the
Green Tree road, off in a clearing; you must see it. A
most lovely spot. Full of Wakefields and Chapleys, Rigbys
and Compsons and Carringtons. Not an ugly tombstone
or monument, and a deferential fringe of cottage worthies.
Always room enough in our cemetery, just a matter of
clearing away more woodland. My older sister's there. It's
through her that Rose Jenner came into the family."

"So I understand."

"Did you ever hear of a feminine chess prodigy before?"

"I never did."

"You ought to have a game with Rose; but her early experience with chess has taken it out of the amusement class for her. Did you know that her father made a living out of her for some time—between her eleventh and fifteenth year?"

"Almost incredible."

" 'Private' meetings, you know; the jaded rich. Well, she's showed no ill effects."

"I believe this tragedy leaves her unprovided for?"

"Well enough provided for; Lydia and I will take care of her. Our circumstances are very much changed, of course—a madman changed them for us. But Rose will be all right."

"Do you know anything about Miss Wakefield's guests, Mr. Carrington?"

"Nothing about the Silvers; they seem decent ordinary people, from the glimpses I've had of them. Silver's connected with some small college. We know old Tom Compson, of course. I'm glad he wasn't here on Thursday night. If there'd been any serious idea that there was a sane reason for those visits, Compson alone would explode it. His money all goes to his university. As for Hattie Bluett—! I'm glad that lock was out of order—the lock on her Library screen door."

He straightened, and faced Gamadge. "We'll see you this evening?"

"Of course, and thank you very much for your help. Tell your sister I greatly appreciate—"

"She's the grateful one."

Carrington turned and went down the walk. Gamadge rang, and was admitted by Miss Pepper.

"Hello there," she said. "You still want Miss Studley? She's still on the porch."

"I still want her." Gamadge tried to think up some reason why he should have wanted her. He went into the dining room and through a French window on the right. The big screened porch was comfortably fitted out with a glider, cushioned wicker chairs, and glass tables. Miss Studley sat at a table doing accounts.

"First of the month coming," she explained, "and income tax instalment two weeks away."

"It isn't good for your patients to listen to that kind of thing." Gamadge leaned up against the doorframe. "I wanted to know whether I could get vitamins in the drugstore here."

"I'm afraid you can't. Sometimes they have some."

"Vitamin B_2."

"I'm sure not those."

"I'll drive in to Westbury tomorrow for them."

"Somebody will be going in from here. Have you the prescription?"

"No, but I know just what they look like. Amber beads the size of a small pea."

"Your doctor won't like you to buy medicine that way!"

"I know the size of the little brutes. Oh—I shan't be in to dinner tonight, Miss Studley."

"Won't you? I'm sorry."

"Funniest thing you know—I find I'm acquainted with Lawrence Carrington."

"No!" Miss Studley's eyes gleamed with interest.

"He evidently heard somehow that I was here—"

"News travels fast in Frazer's Mills. Everybody knows you're here by this time."

"Interested in strangers, are they?"

"Wildly interested, especially now."

"Well, he heard, and he came along to ask me to supper tonight. Until I saw him I didn't realize that he was the Carrington I run into at my club. Perhaps I never knew his first name. I rather hesitated to accept."

"You'll cheer them up. Poor things."

"So he seemed to think."

"And the body's at Westbury."

Gamadge, taken aback by this nonchalance, which he supposed professional, said that he had assumed it was.

"Be sure to tell us tomorrow what that Jenner girl's

like. She's never in the village. Hardly anybody's spoken to her."

"I'll tell you all about her."

Gamadge went back through the house and left it by the side door. He followed a path around to the front, but noted that it was possible to walk on turf all the way.

He strolled across the street and past a group of the cottages; some were of whitewashed brick, some of wood; the first kind very plain, one or two of the latter with scrollwork around the edge of roof and porch. He saw Miss Studley's latticed birthplace. All the cottages had ~rdens, grown and overgrown with dahlias, zinnias and asters. Their doors were closed.

Gamadge crossed the street again and walked up a broad flagged path to the Wakefield Inn. He found the front porch occupied by two young men; one, his chair tilted back against the wall on the house, had rumpled hair and wore spectacles; a book was open on his knees. The other, facing him and seated on the railing, was Garston Yates.

Yates glanced casually at Gamadge and looked away again. The young man in spectacles—he was certainly well under twenty—favored Gamadge with a stare.

Gamadge paused on the top step. "Miss Wakefield at home, do you know?"

The young man in spectacles said: "She was a few minutes ago. She ought to be still, she's entertaining company. You're the new inmate at Studley's."

"Grapevine in good working order, I see." Gamadge smiled at him.

"The hired man stopped by with the big news. It's big news when anybody's fearless enough to come to Frazer's Mills. You're Mr. Gamadge."

He made as if to tilt his chair forward. Gamadge said: "Don't disturb yourself."

The young man looked at Yates. "Perhaps I'd better introduce myself. Fearless as he is, he may not care to stick around when he realizes that I'm at large."

Yates lifted his shoulders, disclaiming any part of this.

The young man addressed Gamadge again: "I'm Silver."

"Are you? Very glad to meet you, Mr. Silver."

"You don't blench. Haven't they told you that I'm the monster?"

10. MONSTERS

"Really?" Gamadge leaned against a post and lighted a cigarette.

"This is Yates," Silver told him, "one of my near-victims. I'll get him yet."

Gamadge and Yates exchanged a brief nod.

"It's a case of adolescent disturbance," said Silver. "My family's protecting me because they think I'll outgrow it. They want me to go to college, not to the booby hatch. No sense of the duties of citizenship at all."

Yates said in a tone of fatigue: "All this, Mr. Gamadge, is because Master Silver was asked a few routine questions by the sheriff and the police."

"Nonsense," said Silver. "I guess I know whether I'm a monster or not; my object was extermination."

"You do seem to have been catholic in your tastes in victims," said Gamadge.

"Well, even I have preferences. I mistook old Mrs. Norbury's room for Mrs. Turnbull's. You've seen Mrs. Turnbull, I suppose? She embodies in her own person the whole meaning of the theory of Conspicuous Waste. Better dead; better dead."

"Drastic," objected Gamadge.

"I mean to be. As for Bluett, the last time I was at the Library looking for something to read, she offered me *Twenty Thousand Leagues under the Sea.*"

"Oh, has she that there? I'd certainly like another go at that," said Gamadge.

"Oh well," said Mr. Silver tolerantly, "some people never do develop in certain directions. When I took out

The Düsseldorf Monster she asked me if I really thought I'd better have it."

"Reading up on yourself, are you?"

Young Silver, dropping his labored fantasy, tilted his chair forward with a bang. He pointed to the book on his knees. "Do you know anything about these monsters?" he asked.

"About as much as you do, I suppose."

"You notice I'm sitting with my back to the wall. It isn't by accident. I'm that way metaphorically until they catch the real monster or let us out of this. It's merely silly to talk about a search; think of all the old cellar foundations and hollow oaks in these woods. This monster is just like the Düsseldorf Monster, and he was the worst in history. Men, women and children, morning, noon or night, it was all the same to him. The city was practically under quarantine for ages. And when they did find him —when they *did* find him, do you know what he was like?"

Gamadge opened his mouth to assent, but young Silver was not to be beaten to his climax:

"He was a harmless little guy, really harmless between bouts, perfectly respectable, and just like anybody."

"They seem to have all kinds of things in the Rigby Library," remarked Gamadge. "I really must go there."

"And do you know what they did to this Düsseldorf maniac?" asked Silver. "They chopped his head off. Doesn't that seem a funny thing to you?"

"You mean it ought to have been looked at as a case of diminished responsibility?"

"Why not? It wasn't so long ago. What were the psychiatrists thinking of? In Germany, too, where they're supposed to have been so up in all that kind of thing."

"Well, it's a difficult problem. Very difficult. A person's supposed to be legally sane if he can exercise control and ingenuity and foresight and so on. The Düsseldorf Monster was very careful. Courts don't like—"

"That isn't the sensible approach to the thing. And in this case, look at the risks! Not much foresight here."

Gamadge looked across the lawn to his left, where the

Rigby hedges rose. He said: "I wonder if Miss Bluett could be persuaded to take me into the Library. Too nervous?"

Young Silver burst out laughing. "Nervous? Bluett? She's there now."

"Is she?"

"Pasting labels on the new consignment, and the Stapler kid's sitting on the doorstep with a baseball bat."

"Well, good for Miss Bluett."

"You notice the poetic justice?" inquired Silver. "A baseball bat is a log of wood."

Yates observed that very young people were so detached.

Gamadge asked: "Did everybody know that Mr. Compson had gone away, Mr. Silver?"

Silver blinked. "Compson? Oh. You mean did everybody think he was in his room Thursday night. Yes, they did; so far as they thought about it at all. Usually his annual trip to Cape Cod is like a durbar. You know he's a descendant of one of the originals? They line up both sides of the street to see him off. But he drove off early on Thursday instead of Friday, some complication about trains, and we were all very much surprised when this transient here showed up instead. A little chiseling on the part of Miss Wakefield, I'm afraid."

"Keep off her," said Yates, without emphasis.

"Your sense of humor is in abeyance. Anyway, off he went; no fanfare, no peasantry gathered round his car to tuck the rugs in. I'll tell you one thing: if I were the Monster I wouldn't have killed old Carrington. What a type! Used to come walking down the street like the king of the Cannibal Islands; kind word for everybody."

"No conspicuous waste there?" Gamadge smiled.

"Nothing bourgeois, nothing for show, all functional to old Carrington. You couldn't blame him for conspicuous waste any more than you could blame a peacock for its tail. Intelligent, too, in his way. We had a lot of interesting chats about N.Y. history. He knew this part of the world like a book, from geology to bugs."

A harassed-looking man of scholarly appearance opened the front door, pushed the screen, and looked out. He said: "Dickie, your mother wants to know where you are."

"Right where you see me, Dad."

"Remember we absolutely forbid you to go off alone in the woods again."

Young Silver nodded glumly.

"You might go down to the drugstore and get her some pop. Get two bottles while you're about it."

Young Silver rose, went over and accepted coins from his father, and then descended the steps. Mr. Silver withdrew.

As young Silver crossed the lawn Yates said out of the side of his mouth: "Great bunch of conspirators, are they not?"

"Yes. Ludicrous."

"Rose is in there."

"In with Miss Wakefield?"

"Yes. First time I've seen her since it happened. We had no chance for a word, with the Monster here."

Gamadge laughed. "Amusing brat."

"He's dying to get off with a posse."

"Are you waiting for a word with Miss Jenner?"

"Don't think she'll give me one. She's evidently here for Lydia Carrington; she said something as she went in."

"I'll go in myself."

"What's your reason for seeing Miss Wakefield? General information?"

"I'm inquiring about rooms."

Yates looked blank. He said after a moment: "Rose looks as if the thing had half killed her. She looks frightful. Have you—have you *any*thing?"

"I've been here a little over three hours."

Gamadge went to the door and rang. A plain woman whose hair was fuzzy from a recent shampoo answered the bell. She smiled at Gamadge austerely.

"Miss Wakefield?"

"I'm Miss Homans, a guest. The women servants are

not allowed by their families to come to Frazer's Mills. But it's all right for *us* to be here." Miss Homans gave a short laugh. "To alibi one another, you know. Idiocy."

Gamadge said: "What a shame. You're the lady who was washing her hair, aren't you?"

"I am. My hair and I have been in every newspaper in the United States. Is there anything particularly funny in a shampoo? You'd think so; I provide comic relief to the case, I believe. It's too bad I didn't invite the Silver boy to sit and entertain me while I washed my hair on Thursday night; you'd suppose I was quite remiss in not having done so. And look at me! Who's to wave me in this place?"

Gamadge smiled politely.

"You'll find Miss Wakefield in her office." Miss Homans stood aside. "I suppose you're not from a newspaper? Those boys promised that they wouldn't let any more newspapers through."

"I shouldn't think they'd want to get farther than young Mr. Silver and Mr. Yates."

"I didn't mean them; I meant the state police."

"Oh, I see. I'm Miss Studley's new inmate."

"Mr. Gamadge; then it's all right."

Miss Homans, looking very curious, showed Gamadge to the doorway of a room at the rear of the hall, and went away. Gamadge stood on the sill until Miss Wakefield, at her desk, looked up and saw him. A girl sat beside her, elbow on the desk and head supported by her hand. Her eyes were half-closed, as if the lids were heavy, but the eyes were brilliant. When she opened them to look at Gamadge he noticed their peculiar color—neither hazel nor gray, yellowish. She was very pale.

Gamadge introduced himself. "I wanted to ask about rooms for later in the year, Miss Wakefield. I have a small family, and I thought this would be the very place for us all to stay in October. Must be lovely in the autumn. My little boy is three; I don't suppose Miss Studley takes young children."

"Sit down, Mr. Gamadge." Miss Wakefield looked at him doubtfully. "My guests do thin out in October, but —you wouldn't want your family here until this trouble is settled."

"It will be, of course."

Rose Jenner got up. She said: "Then I'll tell Lydia, Miss Wakefield." From the moment that she had heard Gamadge's name she had sat motionless, frozen. She had not looked at him again.

"Tell her of course, Rose; of course. We'll have plenty of flowers," said Miss Wakefield.

Gamadge said: "This is Miss Jenner? I found out a little while ago that I know Lawrence Carrington."

"You do?" Miss Wakefield was surprised.

"Yes; he came to Edgewood to speak to me. Miss Carrington sent word that I was to have supper there this evening."

"Lawrence told us, when he—when he heard you were at Edgewood," said Rose.

"Then I'll see you again."

"Yes. I'm glad you can come."

She went out of the room slowly. Miss Wakefield, looking after her, shook her head. "It's been a horrible thing for that child. She was devoted to George Carrington. She found him, you know."

"Yes. Horrible."

"She's not herself at all."

Gamadge sat opposite Miss Wakefield's desk. "I want to write to my wife about this idea of mine," he said. "You do think you'll have rooms for us?"

"I'll have the rooms."

Miss Wakefield's study was large, and it contained besides the littered desk and some well-worn furniture a collection of toys and fancywork displayed on tables. The objects seemed homemade. Gamadge's eye was caught by a large cinnamon-colored animal with stiff whiskers and a baleful look on its snouted face. He got up to examine it.

"I really must have this," he said.

Miss Wakefield glanced at it without favor. "You like it?"

"It would keep me awake at night, but my son has stronger nerves. He'll be delighted with it. He may know whether it's a dog or a bear. Or a monkey? Rabbit? It looks like something from the island of Doctor Moreau."

"I'll wrap it up for you. The things were made here for the Library fund sale." Miss Wakefield rose and got paper and string. She looked at the tag on the animal, and remarked rather disapprovingly: "Two dollars."

"May I contribute an extra dollar to the Library fund? I'd certainly pay three in New York for something not half so original."

"Thanks. Everything helps. Glad to get rid of it." She wrapped the large bundle. Gamadge received it into his arms, and they sat down on opposite sides of her desk. He liked Miss Wakefield.

"Here's my price list. You can write to me." She handed him a typed paper.

"Thanks very much."

Miss Wakefield rubbed the back of her cropped head. She said: "I'm glad you're going up to the Carringtons' this evening. They've behaved very kindly to me about this tragedy. When you see them I wish you'd say something about the way I feel—I never can express myself properly when I feel upset."

"I will of course. I only know Lawrence, Miss Wakefield."

"Poor Lydia, you'll meet a ghost instead of her best self. She represses her feelings too, only she's worse off than I am because she doesn't bang things around the way I do when things go wrong. If I'd only called them up as soon as the Yates boy told me about the axe; I'd have saved George Carrington's life."

"So far as I know anything about it, you behaved as anyone would."

"The Yates boy was so sure it was somebody in the house—somebody belonging here. I knew that was ridiculous, but he hypnotized me into thinking the tramp might be hiding here, and so we searched the house first. It wasn't his fault—a stranger couldn't know the geography of the place, and how close the Carringtons are. How close we all are to one another, for the matter of that. I'm glad those traveling men got away—it's so hard on people of that sort when these things happen. You're always afraid they may have been up to some silly little kind of misbehavior or other, and then they're suddenly in the limelight and get found out."

Gamadge said: "That Yates fellow seems a nice kind of boy. I had a word or two with him on the porch."

Miss Wakefield gave him a quick look. "He is—very nice fellow indeed. He's been most considerate all the way through; no fussing or complaining, and actually helps me out in the kitchen."

"You knew the late Mr. Carrington well, of course; his death must be a good deal of a loss to you all."

"Well, you might say I knew him; but I wasn't a contemporary. Too young for him, too old for Lawrence and Lydia. Our families were always intimate here, but after I left school we stayed in The Mills the year round. The Carringtons only came up for a month or two in the summer, and now and then at Christmas."

"Interesting personality, George Carrington's, I gather."

"Not particularly interesting; very attractive to some people. I don't care much for these old Turks myself."

"Turks?" Gamadge was amused.

"Women's place is the parlor, if it isn't in the laundry and the kitchen. Lydia should have been encouraged to play the piano in public. No man was good enough for her, or for Nadine either; so Nadine went and married Jenner and Lydia never married at all. She ought to have had a big interest in life to take the place of all that. Then George started mewing Rose Jenner up in the same way."

"Mewing her up? She could drive all over the countryside alone—"

"That's nothing; who can't, nowadays? That was no substitute for young friends and young men. They had plenty of company themselves. But nobody was good enough for Rose Jenner—the old story. Not that *she* ever complained—the Carringtons are perfect, to Rose Jenner. But she's a spirited girl, has a lot more spirit than Lydia ever had. I shouldn't have been a bit surprised if Carrington had had another elopement on his hands sooner or later. Well, nobody cares now what she does, poor little thing. I used to ask her here when my guests had little parties for the young people; but there was always some excuse. I hope she saw a little life at boarding school, but I don't think so; any boarding school Carrington picked out would see that she didn't."

"Carrington was the complete egoist, was he?"

"Yes, but he had his good points, as his behavior about taking Rose Jenner in shows. It meant spending money out of his income. That annuity—they all insist it was a good thing, gave them all a better life, and I'd have given George Carrington at least twenty years more myself; but I don't think he bought that annuity for anyone's sake but his own. Not George Carrington. He spent right up to the income; told me so only this summer. Didn't even have insurance—catch him paying out the premiums!"

She paused, drummed on the table, and frowned. Gamadge reflected gloomily that those knotty fingers and strong hands, those bony wrists, could probably control the biggest bay that ever came out of the Wakefield training stables; that Miss Wakefield's long legs were probably equipped with muscles as good, and powerful knees. What a waste. He would have liked to see Miss Wakefield astride a good big bay horse. Or would she ride sidesaddle? There was plenty of science in that, too, and more danger.

"Rose is badly worried about Lydia," she said. "I wish to goodness you'd see what you think, and let me know; tell me if you think Lydia's in for a breakdown."

"I'll try to observe." Gamadge rose. "Thank you very much, Miss Wakefield, for offering me rooms; and I'll write to my wife. We're booked for October."

"I hope you'll come." Miss Wakefield got out of her chair springily. "And I hope Mrs. Gamadge doesn't count on gaiety. One little boy, you say?"

"Yes. My wife will like it here, although we're not a middle-aged couple. Don't judge her by me, you know." Gamadge smiled. "My wife is beautiful and young, as—er—the young Flora in her prime. Am I quoting or did I make that up? Probably I made it up, it's a trifle tautological."

Miss Wakefield laughed. "Gives me the idea, anyhow."

Gamadge, shifting the Monster from one arm to the other, asked diffidently: "Would I be making myself out too much of a sensation collector if I said I'd like to see the celebrated side door, Miss Wakefield?"

"Not at all; everybody wants to see it. The trouble is, there's nothing to see. They took the axe, I don't know why."

"Gives them *something*."

"To look at, I suppose. Or they may think we'll kill one another with it after all." She led the way through a door in the north wall into a narrow corridor. It was cut by a cross passage, and Gamadge stood in this passage and looked along it to the door that now opened on greenness and sunshine. Then he turned and glanced at the back stairs, and at the brackets above the fire buckets where the axe had hung.

"My curiosity is slaked," he said.

"You're more easily satisfied than some. That's Mr. Compson's room, just along there. We'll go to the front through the parlor."

They did so, and she left him at the front door. On the porch, Gamadge exchanged a word with Yates:

"Your landlady's sticking by you."

"Nice woman. Wish I could tell her the whole thing."

"Wouldn't be fair to saddle her with the responsibility."

"Rose didn't say a word to me when she left."

"Of course she didn't. Your Miss Jenner is no fool."

"Gamadge—you can't judge, seeing her now; but don't

105

you think she seems very tense—under an awful strain?"

"Her reaction to strangers isn't sympathetic. I thought that might account for the tension."

"How could it? I suppose Miss Carrington is sapping her vitality. Simply collapsing on her. As for you—I wish she'd known you were here on our account."

"Your account."

"It's the same thing."

"She's not to be told, you know; nobody's to be told why I'm here. That's understood."

"I wouldn't put that responsibility on her, any more than I'd put it on Miss Wakefield." He added, as Gamadge went down the steps: "What's that thing you're carrying?"

"I don't know."

11. CRIMINOLOGY

Gamadge went down to the street, turned right and passed the Tavern. A few people were in the drugstore. He walked on. A thick grove of lilac bushes. hid the rear premises of the Tavern, ending at the hedge that bounded the Library domain. Beyond it came the shadowy lawn of the Rigby place; he turned up the winding path.

The path took him around to the north, where a half-grown youth sat on the doorstep reading. His baseball bat was lying beside him.

He looked up. "Name and occupation," he said, "and cards of identity."

"Gamadge. Document man." Gamadge solemnly fumbled for his wallet. Willie Stapler read what was on the blue card, and looked at Gamadge's fingerprints with a knowing air. "Where'd you get this?"

"Somebody required me to fill it out during the war."

"Fingerprints too?"

"As you see. Rather a nice idea, don't you think? Now I can't commit any crimes."

The Stapler boy searched for the gap in this reasoning, abandoned the search, and returned the card. He asked: "Business here?"

"Something to read. I heard Miss Bluett was on the premises."

"You're at Studley's."

"That's right."

The Stapler boy got up, went into the Library, and came back with a square-faced, square-bodied woman who

107

looked at Gamadge sharply through pince-nez. She said: "Not open for business."

"I know, Miss Bluett, but I'm a kind of writer, and I thought you might be willing to allow me to look at an encyclopedia. I want some data on Aubrey, the melodious twang man."

Miss Bluett said after a pause: "Well, come in. Reference shelves to the right."

Gamadge followed her into the cool depths of the big room, found his volume, and laid it out on a shelf. Miss Bluett stood contemplating him for a few moments; the kind of person, thought Gamadge, who won't ask questions.

She retreated to her alcove. Gamadge had placed his bundle on a chair when he came in; he left it where it was, after he had replaced the encyclopedia, and wandered along looking at books.

Miss Bluett was surrounded by the Carrington donation. Gamadge, having completed his tour of the north and west walls, approached her diffidently and picked a small octavo, bound in peach-colored cloth, from the nearest pile.

"*Mr. Isaacs,*" he said, "and I haven't seen the old boy for a quarter of a century. How pretty covers used to be. Would it be too much for me to ask you to make me out a card, so I could take this back to Edgewood with me?"

Miss Bluett twitched *Mr. Isaacs* out of his hand, inspected it, and said: "All right, I've done this one." She placed it on her desk and got out her pencil with the rubber stamp on the end of it. She took a library card out of a rack.

"References? Miss Studley will do."

"I was going to say Lawrence Carrington."

Miss Bluett was also one of the people who don't like assistance when doing their job. But she was too much interested in the news that Gamadge knew Carrington to be really annoyed. She repeated: "Lawrence Carrington?"

"I know him a little. I'm having supper with them."

"Oh." Miss Bluett snatched up an eraser and rubbed out what she had begun to write on the reference line. She took Gamadge's New York Public Library card from him and copied down what it said. "Going to stay here long?" she asked.

"Not long. Lovely little place."

"Hope it'll cure you of what's the trouble."

"Just overwork," said Gamadge obligingly.

Miss Bluett stamped *Mr. Isaacs* and pushed it at Gamadge. Picking it up, he reflected that she was wasted on Frazer's Mills. No scope.

"Two weeks, renewal if necessary, five cents a day overtime," she told him, and took another Carrington book from a pile.

Gamadge moved along to the south wall. "Nice stuff here," he said. "I'm rather sorry tomorrow's a holiday and you'll be closed up. But you won't agree with me about that."

Miss Bluett could no longer allow this fool to imagine that nothing had happened at the Rigby Library. She said shortly: "I might as well work. They won't let me take my holiday."

Gamadge swung to her and spoke incredulously: "You mean you can't leave town because you thought you heard the murderer at the door on Thursday night?"

Miss Bluett rose to this promptly and with vigor: "I did hear him at the door Thursday night, and saw him too. I don't know that I'd have mentioned it if I'd known I'd lose my trip."

"Of course you would have mentioned it." Gamadge came and leaned against the front of her desk. "Public servant like you—of course you'd mention it. What an experience. Terrifying."

"Not terrifying at all, because I thought it was a moth or a squirrel." She paused. "All I saw moving away was a shadow. And I needn't have been here at all so late if it hadn't been for this junk." She cast a disgusted look at the rampart of Carrington books. "Nice thing to nearly lose your life for."

"No good?"

"The first two lots aren't so bad. I wish I'd never made Hawkins go for that last load on Thursday evening, but I didn't know when I could get him to take his truck out again. He's supposed to take entire care of the Library, and it's a full-time job, and he's paid for it; but he does odd work besides in summer. We have hardly anybody for that kind of thing in The Mills—clipping hedges and mowing grass; only Miss Wakefield's help and Carrington's man Begbie, and Miss Studley's chauffeur. And Hawkins is so dumb. He had to go and leave a book behind after all."

"Leave a book?"

Miss Bluett jerked her head to the left. "One of those bird books. It's a set of twelve, and he only brought eleven. Maddening."

Gamadge picked up the top book of the set—a thin quarto, nicely bound in green cloth and decorated with stampings of gold. He read: *Birds of Our Woodlands*.

"Regional birds?" Gamadge opened it, and a colored plate of *The Blue-jay* fell out. "Nice set. Too bad if the plates are loose."

"The plates! That set's ruined. Covers falling off, pages dog-eared, engravings torn. Hundreds of children been at it."

Gamadge clapped the covers of the quarto, and dust flew. He picked up others and went on clapping.

"Don't do that," said Miss Bluett, "you'll get dust all over the place. Hawkins does that. The Carringtons never cared about books; only the man that bought the Library, and now Lawrence. At least they tell me Lawrence does, but he never comes in here. Lydia comes now and then to get a current novel, and that Jenner girl is always in here reading. But she's no relation. Horses and dogs, fishing and shooting, that's all the Carringtons cared about."

Gamadge had ceased from his labors. He stacked the Woodland Birds again and looked at some of the other piles, bending sideways.

"Miss Jenner's a reader?" he asked. "From what I've heard I shouldn't have thought so."

"More for something to do than anything else, I guess. She doesn't take books out, just sits here and looks through things. The only book she ever asked for was *Chess Strategics.*" Miss Bluett glanced at him crossly. "*Chess Strategics!*"

Gamadge straightened, dusted his hands off, and shook his head.

"And when I said we didn't have it, she said never mind, she only wanted to show Mr. Carrington something. Evidently she knew it by heart."

"Extraordinary." Gamadge returned to the west side of the Library and looked along a shelf that he had noticed before. He said: "Criminology; always interesting."

"I call them morbid."

"Morbid? Here's the Tichborne Case, of all things. Trials aren't morbid, Miss Bluett."

"I mean those crime books."

"But you get such wonderful contemporary detail, and you don't get it anywhere else; not in memoirs, or letters, or even journals. Only in crime books, and above all in murder cases. Everything comes out in a murder case, all the trivia that are never recorded anywhere else. And why?"

Gamadge, *The Tichborne Trial* in his hands, looked earnestly at Miss Bluett.

"Well, why?" She was mildly amused by this easy-mannered stranger who had handled *Birds of Our Woodlands* so tenderly.

"Because in a trial for murder the simplest annals of the middle class and the poor suddenly become of the first importance—they're weapons in a battle of life and death. They're handled like jewels—by the judge, who's so particular; by counsel, who are so persistent; by witnesses, who rack their brains and talk their heads off. Old or new, Star Chamber or jury trial, out it all comes —the recipe for soups, fatal or otherwise; the way to

111

make a fire; the medical treatment for that vague ailment that turned out to be the effects of laurel water."

"Laurel water?"

"Very bad for you."

"What's laurel water?"

"Now, Miss Bluett, don't be morbid."

Miss Bluett found herself laughing.

"Why, if this murder case, the Carrington murder case, ever comes to trial," Gamadge went on, "or even if it doesn't, even if it ends up as a Great Unsolved Crime, you'll be immortal. A hundred years from now people may be reading all about you—you and the Rigby Library, the holiday you never got, the bird book that Hawkins didn't bring, the catch on the door that slipped and saved your life. Intellectual curiosity isn't morbid."

Miss Bluett said: "You're making a mistake about my never getting my holiday. I'm going to get it, all right, don't worry. I'm going away after the inquest for a good long rest."

"Fine. And I suppose you'll be closed up tomorrow. Nice for you, but I must say I wish I could come back here before I leave. Lots of things I'd like to look at again." He replaced *The Tichborne Trial.* "This, for instance. Fascinating detail, even if it was only a trial about a claim to an estate. The claimant was so fat, he—"

Miss Bluett again condescended to laugh. "Tell you what," she said after a short hesitation, "you seem to know how to handle books, and you're a friend of Lawrence Carrington's. I could let you have my key."

"Miss Bluett, that's really most—"

"Be careful of it, it's the only one except Hawkins' cellar key. Every time you use it you'll have to leave it with Mrs. Stapler."

"Of course." Gamadge accepted the key and put it away in a key case with his others.

"Perhaps you'll clap some more books for me," added Miss Bluett. "You'll do it without tearing the covers off the way Hawkins does, and I won't be here to get the dust all over me."

Gamadge showed appreciation of Miss Bluett's humor.

"Now wouldn't you like to wash your hands? There's a bathroom in back there along the passage next to the kitchen."

"I should like to wash my hands. Why a kitchen, Miss Bluett?"

"This last Rigby fixed the house up for himself and his help. He was a bachelor. Bedrooms upstairs, for them; his bedroom and bathroom down here. Nice kitchen, we didn't do anything about it—it's gone to waste."

"The housing people will get after you and install a family."

"Then I'll resign and the family can run the Library."

Gamadge went back along the passage, from which stairs led up and down. He washed his hands in a large old-fashioned bathroom, and dried them on a paper towel, which he dropped into a metal basket. He came back, thanked Miss Bluett again, hoped he'd still be in Frazer's Mills when she returned from her holiday, and collected *Mr. Isaacs* and the Monster. He went out into the sun and lengthening shadow of the afternoon.

Miss Bluett followed him to the door. She summoned the Stapler boy, who now sat under a tree, and Gamadge left them conversing on the step. He walked down to the street. Nobody was in sight except a state policeman whom Gamadge had not seen before, and who smoked a cigarette in the shade of the Library hedge.

12. ELIMINATIONS

The officer said: "Good afternoon. You're Mr. Gamadge."

"People have been telling me so all day," said Gamadge.

"You're quite famous."

"In one way or another. You're Vines."

"That's right. My beat is at the Edgewood end. Goin' there now."

He went to his motorcycle, which leaned against a tree, righted it, and wheeled it to the curb. Willie Stapler came down across the lawn, a dollar bill in one hand and a slip of paper in the other.

"Hey, sonny," said Vines, "leavin' your post?"

"She latched herself in. Wants some stuff from the drugstore—they close up on Sundays at five."

He turned up the street towards the Tavern. Gamadge and Vines walked in the other direction, Gamadge on the footway and Vines at the curb. Vines said: "Adey thinks all this is a waste of time."

"You don't agree with him?"

"In a way I do. But"—Vines moved his head to the left—"Adey laughs about checking up on those cottages over there."

Gamadge looked across the road at a particularly sweet little house—one with the jigsaw trimmings; he asked: "Does he?"

"Sure. My folks come from Maine."

"They do?"

"Way down in Maine. You ought to hear some of the stories they can tell you about villages there. Not farms

114

way out in the country, you know; villages about the size of this one with the neighbors right on top of you."

"I've heard stories."

"No, but the folks have one about a house in some small town, and one day a neighbor happened in around suppertime, when it ain't considered just the thing to go dropping in."

"I know," said Gamadge, laughing.

"Went in the back way. There was a woman—girl—sitting at the kitchen table being fed some supper. Fat girl. One of the family, that was sure—there hadn't been visitors. This neighbor had never seen this girl before, never heard of her, didn't know there was any such person in the house. Far as the town knew, there never had been."

"Creepy."

"The neighbor went through to the front, said what she had to say, beat it out front. Nobody ever mentioned the fat girl, and nobody ever heard of her again. Died, I suppose, and they carted her off in the middle of the night and buried her."

"They know how to mind their own business down that way."

"Don't they though? Plenty of gab, but where does it get to? Perhaps they know how to mind their own business in Frazer's Mills; it ain't a place like any other."

"Unique, I should say."

"Closed corporation. I'll tell you one house got searched that night, and by me." He added: "And it proves my point."

"Edgewood?"

"That got a pretty good going over, too; I'm talking about Carringtons'. In spite of the fact that the feller's footprints did lead away from the door, I was nervous about Carringtons'. It's a big house, closed most of the year. Plenty of facilities for taking care of funny folks in the attics. So I asked permission, and I went through the place. And even so, if it hadn't been for Miss Carrington herself, I'd have missed something."

"What?"

Officer Vines screwed up his face and grinned at Gamadge. "Would you think of searching a pediment?"

"A pediment?" Gamadge was astonished.

"That's what they call that triangular part that runs across the front of the house over the porch."

"I know."

"But did you know they could be hollow and have a space in them? This one has. Nobody knows why; perhaps there ought to be a way of getting into them in case of leaks or rats or too many chipmunks. There's a square hole leading into the Carrington's pediment, a square hole at the front end of the upper hall, with a big map hung over it. You'd never imagine. Miss Carrington showed me—Lawrence reminded her, she said."

"Interesting. So you looked in there?"

"Nothing, of course, but it shows you. Those little old houses might have any kind of hide-holes in them; space under the rafters, behind a chimney. Adey says not."

"No wonder they all lock up, if your delightful idea is a possibility."

"They lock up, all right; they all bolt themselves into their bedrooms at night, even the Carringtons do. Miss Carrington told Mrs. Begbie. Or was it Mrs. Begbie told Miss Carrington to do it?"

"That way, I imagine."

They had reached the Edgewood drive. Vines said: "Well, be seeing you."

"How do you manage about relief and so on?"

"We eat at Mrs. Broadbent's—the Tavern. Adey and I work here from midmorning till around eleven at night. Hope it won't keep up forever."

"The inquest will change things a little."

"So they say."

Vines got on his motorcycle and rode up the Green Tree road. Gamadge turned into the Edgewood grounds; Miss Studley, busy in a flower garden at one side of the lawn, waved to him. He saluted in return and went on up the drive. He mounted the steps.

The front door was open; Miss Pepper could be seen in the lounge arranging flowers. She said as Gamadge pushed open the screen: "Tea served on the porch at five, Mr. Gamadge. You'll find Mrs. Turnbull out there now, and I think Mr. Motley."

"Good."

"Been shopping?"

"Just something for the progeny." He unwrapped his bundle, and Miss Pepper exclaimed with delight:

"How cute!"

"A parent speaks."

"I only wish I had one like it for my Billy."

"Miss Wakefield may not be out of them." Gamadge was turning to the stairs when the telephone rang. He waited. Miss Pepper went back to the booth, and returned to say that the call was for him. "And I'll take the—I'll take it upstairs with me."

"It's a panda—the brown ones are rare."

Miss Pepper said that Gamadge was a terror. He went to the booth and picked up the receiver.

"Gamadge?"

"Hello, Durfee."

"That Pennsylvania business."

"Quick work. Yes?"

"I'll give you what I have. Three guests in the house that night besides the servants and Mr. and Mrs. A red-head woman, friend of Mrs. T.'s, and her husband; well-known characters in the city, rich, the Ellwood Garveys. And a man named Matthews, friend of the late Mr. T., brought along to the house party to play bridge. The deceased couldn't get the game through his head."

"Chauffeur friend?"

"No, man that helped the deceased with his financial affairs—which means what Mrs. T. gave him. Dark, good-looking, out of war service on account of some physical disability, been working in Washington. Harold Matthews. Mrs. T. hadn't met him before. He came originally from East Orange."

"Thanks. That'll do."

"Anything for you?"

"Don't think so. Let you know."

"That case is a washout, Gamadge. The deceased never went to bed sober, his valet said, had trouble with his nerves and took sleeping stuff regularly. Of course it weakened on him, and he overdid it. His doctor warned him."

"I understand. Had his own room, you said?"

"I don't know what I said; he had his own room, anyway. Found late next morning. All evidence pointed to the fact that he was attentive to his wife, took her around, acted fond of her. She was happy with him, and if the servants say so it's true. You don't want to make anything of it, do you?"

"Probably not."

"Getting along at all?"

"I wouldn't say so."

"Well, watch **it**."

Gamadge came out of the booth and made his way through the dining room to the porch. He stopped in the doorway. Motley faced it, leaning against the opposite rail; hands in pockets, chin down, he had the look of a man who has come to a dead end.

Mrs. Turnbull reclined on a chaise lounge, so far to the right that she was invisible to anyone not standing where Gamadge stood; a good arrangement. Motley, in fact, said something in a low voice as Gamadge approached, and when he caught sight of her she was picking up a magazine. Her face was composed.

Gamadge looked from one to the other of them; he said: "I think you two must be the greatest idiots on earth."

Motley had lifted his head, and would probably have greeted Gamadge with a casual word; now he stared, mouth half open. Mrs. Turnbull's magazine slowly descended to her lap, and her eyes showed white all around the irises.

"Your name's Harold Matthews," continued Gamadge, ignoring her and addressing Motley, whose color was changing to the queerest grayish pallor. "You were at the Turnbull house in Pittsburgh the night Turnbull died. You were probably a friend of Mrs. Turnbull's, though she and you didn't advertise that fact to her other friends. When she was sent here you had yourself sent too, by a doctor who knows you under a false name. Were you crazy to do such a thing?"

Matthews had trouble in answering. At last he got his lips somewhat under control, and spoke huskily: "How could we know we'd get caught in a damned trap?"

Mrs. Turnbull covered her face with a handkerchief, held in both hands. She faltered through it: "There wasn't any harm. It was only because it didn't look well for us to be up here together so soon afterwards. It isn't Harold's fault. I made him."

Matthews asked through his teeth: "Are you police?"

"No. And you can be thankful I got the information from somebody who tapped a private source. It's not information that your doctor would give out to everybody —perhaps he wouldn't give it out to anyone. But as luck would have it he wasn't in town, and the office nurse obliged with the word that you'd proposed yourself for Edgewood."

"But—I don't see why you asked."

"I asked because I want to eliminate people from suspicion in this case—weed out the impossibles. I was following all pointers. I rather wondered why a man of your age and type—a man, by the way, whose ailment might be a fake—should want to come to Edgewood. If it's any comfort to you and Mrs. Turnbull, you are eliminated from my point of view. Mrs. Turnbull was sent here for a definite reason by her specialist, you came to be with her. Too bad we can't use the material."

Mrs. Turnbull began to sob.

Matthews said violently: "A chance in a million."

"Not quite, Matthews. Or I'd better go on calling you Motley, I suppose. No use risking a slip." Mrs. Turnbull took her handkerchief away from her face and looked at Gamadge with a faint dawning hope in her eyes. He went on: "Not quite such odds as that. You weren't born yesterday. You know the chances—sudden illness, all kinds of coincidences, unexpected meetings—"

"I thought it was safe enough in this hole. They never had my pictures in the papers last June, and May telephoned me that there wasn't anybody here we knew. She's telling you the absolute truth, she just wanted me along for company."

"We thought it was such a joke," quavered Mrs. Turnbull, "nobody knowing we'd ever met before. It was such fun."

"Such fun for Motley to be here under an assumed name—in the circumstances?"

Motley said: "Gamadge—for God's sake you don't think . . . ? Turnbull died of accidental poisoning, his own stuff. Everybody knows it."

"Then why introduce an element of conspiracy afterwards? I'm not investigating Turnbull's death, Motley."

"You're not?"

"No. And to be frank with you, I don't believe either you or Mrs. Turnbull would have run such a risk if you'd been responsible."

"Of course we wouldn't," said Motley, with simulated scorn.

"But others might not argue as I do."

Mrs. Turnbull began to cry again. "I loved Clarence, I was heartbroken. I still am. Harold was the only comfort I had, and I couldn't even see him because everybody thought he was Clarence's friend, and Harold didn't think it was safe."

Harold gave her a glance that did not express affection.

"People *talk* so," wailed Mrs. Turnbull.

"They do." Gamadge stood contemplating her with a certain exasperation.

"And every minute we're here now—"

"The inquest will do it," muttered her friend. "They'll get pictures, and some newshawk will be sure to connect up."

120

"They tried to suggest at the time that somebody might have gone to Clarence's room that night and had a drink with him," said Mrs. Turnbull faintly.

"But there wasn't any motive?" Gamadge turned from her to Motley. "Only one thing possible—to get you out of here before the inquest."

"Don't I know that?"

"You know it. Now of course you've both been keeping out of the limelight as much as possible; you'd even suppress evidence, I suppose, rather than make yourselves conspicuous in the case. You'd even hand out false evidence if necessary. I understand all that; I won't blame you for it. But if I'm to help you out of this—which I probably won't be able to do—you'll both have to be frank with me now. In the first place, can you alibi each other? Were you together on Thursday evening when the party opened Mrs. Norbury's door and then left?"

Mrs. Turnbull reacted violently to this suggestion: "How dare you?"

Motley smiled—a smile of bitterness. "We *would* have been crazy, Gamadge; at that hour. Very little privacy at Edgewood until later, much later, and no guarantee at any time; with hypochondriacs watching their symptoms and waiting for palpitations all night."

Gamadge answered Mrs. Turnbull's implied rebuke: "Of course you'd want to meet sometimes, Mrs. Turnbull; the joke wouldn't be any good if you couldn't share it in private now and then. Nothing in that."

"Harold and I were not together."

"That's that. Your room is at the back, next to Mrs. Norbury's. Motley's, I think, is in front next to mine. Did either of you—"

Motley said: "She thinks she heard the maniac arrive."

"Just a little noise from the direction of the woods," faltered Mrs. Turnbull. "I didn't think anything of it. But afterwards I remembered that I heard it just before half past ten. I happened to look at my watch at half past, to set it by my traveling clock."

And count the hours, thought Gamadge. He said: "Mrs. Norbury didn't hear this noise."

"She's deaf. She doesn't know it, but she's deaf."

"Well, it would have helped to exonerate Edgewood, but I can see that you wouldn't care to come forward."

Mrs. Turnbull sat up, put her feet to the floor, and rose. After a pitiful struggle between resentment and anxiety, she spoke in a tremulous and wheedling voice: "Mr. Gamadge, I don't know what your interest is in all this. But if you can possibly help us, you won't find me ungrateful."

"No, May," said Motley. "Don't offer him anything."

"I mean I'll be grateful to him. I don't want tea; I have a headache, and please tell them I can't be disturbed."

She tottered across the porch, past Gamadge, and away. There was a long silence, during which Gamadge sat down and lighted a cigarette. At last Motley spoke harshly:

"I know what you think. Say it if you want to, I'm in no position to complain."

"Never mind what I think, Mr. Motley. You're in no position to be lectured by me."

"Somebody'll marry her; I'd make her a better husband than that oaf Turnbull did. But I doubt whether she'll ever get up the nerve to marry me now." He added: "Even if we squeak out of this."

"Oh, I don't know," said Gamadge. "After a good long wait you could probably manage it quite openly through mutual friends. It would have to be openly, unless you feel able to risk trouble."

"A good long wait?" Motley laughed. "She'll have the first man that gets a chance at her—if he's moderately presentable. I'm fond of her, you know," he insisted, and his voice was suddenly a whine. "I met her long before Turnbull ever saw her, scraped acquaintance in a teashop. But he was on hand, and he got ahead of me after the old man died. I know it looks funny, my being there the night Turnbull cashed in, but I was the only unattached man she knew, and she had me along to play bridge. Good food, all the liquor you could drink, and May knew I had no money and staked me—none of the rest of them knew that." He paused. "If you've dug into my medical history you know I'm handicapped."

"Yes."

"And I haven't a cent except what I can earn."

"Mrs. Turnbull staked you to the Creighton, I suppose?" Gamadge's tone was a detached one.

"Naturally. The whole idea appealed to her. I was a fool, but I didn't like to disappoint her."

"If it does come out, you realize of course that she'll always be viewed as an accessory; more likely, an accomplice."

"And she'd make such a rotten showing on the witness stand. Gamadge, I don't know why you bother with us; but if there's any earthly chance—"

Heralded by a clinking of silver against glass, Miss Pepper approached through the dining room with a tray. Both men came forward to help her. Haynes followed her, a plate in each hand, and Mrs. Norbury lumbered in his wake.

"Mrs. Turnbull has a headache," said Gamadge. "Lying down. No tea by request."

"What a shame." Miss Pepper arranged the tray. She left them, and Mrs. Norbury settled herself to preside.

"And what have you all been doing?" she asked brightly.

Haynes said: "I tried to take a walk."

"Tried?" Mrs. Norbury passed cups. Haynes, looking gloomily into his, nodded. "Along that wood path. Game wardens—bah! There was somebody walking along parallel to me in the woods."

Everybody looked at him.

"And why *not* a game warden?" inquired Mrs. Norbury, still brightly.

"Fellow would have spoken when I called out. He didn't. Went on towards Wakefield's. I cut down between

Wakefield's and the Library, through all that jungle of thorn bushes." He glanced down at his tweeds and picked vegetation from his knee.

Mrs. Norbury asked less brightly: "Did you speak to the police officers?"

"Neither of 'em in sight, and that deputy went off to supper long ago. Their hours are incredible." He swallowed some tea and went on: "I suppose they searched that empty house—the school?"

"Of course," said Motley. "Went through it Thursday night, in spite of the fact that it was locked up tight as a drum. When did you hear this fellow in the woods, Mr. Haynes?"

"About half an hour ago. Dare say it was some native, or one of those boys looking for trouble. But the place gets on your nerves. I had my walk up and down the street. There comes that motorcycle fellow now. I suppose I ought to have a word with him."

There was a chugging from the Green Tree road, and they heard the motorcycle pass. It stopped beyond Edgewood. Haynes finished his tea and got up.

"Getting sick of it," he said.

"Your tramp's reached the millpond by now," Motley told him. "Why start another panic? The sooner it all dies down the better for us."

Haynes sat down again and took a piece of bread and butter.

"How about a game tonight?" asked Mrs. Norbury. "If Mrs. Turnbull isn't up to it, Mr. Gamadge will take a hand. What do you play for, Mr. Gamadge? Is a quarter of a cent too low for you?"

Gamadge said it wasn't. They sat silent after that, even Mrs. Norbury at a loss for conversation. But it was she, deaf though she may have been, who first looked up, turned her head, and remarked that there was something going on down the street. Old ears are tuned to calamity.

Everybody looked to the left, but the screen and the trees beyond cut them off from any view of street or Library. There was certainly a sound of voices somewhere in that direction, a shout, and then a sudden sharp cry. In another moment a woman was screaming. The three men on the porch got to their feet.

13. TRIUMPH OF VINES

Mrs. Norbury, looking very froglike in her dismay, stayed where she was; Motley got as far as the front door, thought better of it, and remained there; Miss Studley, loyal to her post, went no farther than the porch steps, where she stood and shouted after Miss Pepper to come right back and tell her what the trouble was. Haynes couldn't run on account of his heart, so Miss Pepper, with Gamadge close behind, were the only people from Edgewood to dash across the lawn and down to the street. Gamadge overtook Miss Pepper as she rounded the library hedge.

The oldest inhabitants, and the fattest ones, were still streaming across the road and up to the Library; a crowd was already there, going on around it to the back. The screaming had stopped. A middle-aged woman, tears on her distorted face, stood on the Library path; somebody paused beside her and addressed her as Mrs. Stapler.

Dick Silver ran past Gamadge, who caught at his arm; the arm was snatched away, and the Silver boy galloped on towards the Wakefield Inn. Two motorcycles, abandoned in haste, leaned against the curb.

Gamadge ran up the lawn, dodging shrubs and trees. The front door of the Library was closed, the casement windows high; he went around to the rear and found the crowd surging about the cellar steps, with Vines keeping them back. When he saw Gamadge he beckoned to him; there was a curious look of triumph in the policeman's eye.

"What is it?" Gamadge was panting.

126

"He got Miss Bluett."

"How? When?"

"While you and me were talking down on the street. While the Stapler kid was getting her things for her at the drugstore."

"I don't—"

"Sure, she was locked in. Don't you get it? He was here all the time."

"Here?" Gamadge looked vacantly up at the peaked roof of the Rigby house.

"Up on the second floor. He's been here ever since Thursday night. Left a nest of newspapers and some bread crumbs and stuff." Vines smiled. "What did I say?"

"You mean nobody ever searched the Library?"

"I guess it's one on us, but why would we search the Library? He didn't even go in the Library, why should we imagine he'd come back? But he did come back."

"How did he get in?"

"Ask the Stapler kid."

Willie Stapler, his face pale and frightened, was standing on the fringe of the crowd. He came slowly forward. Gamadge looked at him blankly.

"She didn't lock up after herself Thursday night," he said. "When we came over here today the door wasn't locked, and I saw it wasn't, and she told me."

"Told you she didn't lock up when you left with her on Thursday night?"

"She pretended she forgot her torch, she said that was why she sent over for me to take her home; but I knew then she was scared, and she was too scared to remember to lock up."

"Did she say so this afternoon?"

"No, but she was embarrassed. She said: 'Of all things, I never locked up.'"

"I see."

Vines took up the story: "And the feller's had three quarters of an hour to get away—if he's gone."

"Mr. Haynes heard somebody in the woods; here he is, he'll tell you."

Haynes came up, and told Vines what he had heard. Vines gave a short laugh: "We might have caught him, all right."

"If you'd been here," said Haynes.

"We wasn't far. Well, so you heard him going off in a southerly direction. Get him yet, perhaps; Adey's telephoning in there. This time there *will* be a cordon."

Gamadge put his hand into a breast pocket and got out his key case: "She gave me her key."

"That so?" Vines took it without surprise. "We thought she had it."

"So that I could get in and read while she was away."

"And Hawkins had the only other one—cellar key." He glanced behind him, down the steps, to the open door. "He let us in."

"How did you—"

"This Stapler boy came back with the drugs for her, and found the front door shut and locked as he left it. He couldn't make her hear, thought she might be back in the bathroom, or upstairs. So he just sat down under his tree and forgot about it."

"I did not forget," said Willie Stapler. "I knew she'd be coming out pretty soon; she lives with us, she always comes home a few minutes after five. I waited, and I was doing my summer school reading; little while ago I banged on the front door again, I knew Mom would be expecting me. When she didn't answer I went and told Mom, and Mom went across and got Charlie Hawkins. He let us in." Willie Stapler turned his white face to Gamadge. "It was a log of wood off the cellar pile."

"That's so," said Vines. "That's what he likes to use —log of wood."

"Was that Mrs. Stapler screaming?"

"She couldn't help it," said Willie, his lip trembling.

"I should think not."

Vines said: "Adey's telephoning the sheriff. Just as well the front door was locked, these folks would have been all over the place." He glanced after Haynes, who had turned away to repeat his story to somebody in the crowd. Then he asked Gamadge in a low voice: "You want in?"

"Yes."

"I got to stay here. There's Hawkins now, he can help me with the bunch here."

Hawkins came through from the cellar and mounted the steps; an oldish man, who looked haggard. Adey was behind him.

"Barracks notified, sheriff coming," said Adey.

"Take Mr. Gamadge in, will you?" said Vines.

Gamadge went down the steps, and past Adey into the dark of the cellar. Dampness rose from the earth floor, oozed through the ancient foundations. Adey shut and bolted the door behind them and flashed his torch.

"Careful of that firewood," he said. "Some of it rolled when he took the log off."

They circled the pile of maple logs and went across to the cellar stairs.

"He walked easy," said the officer. "I don't see footprints, but we better keep to the edge of the stairs and the upper hall." They mounted the steep flight. Gamadge found himself in the back passage; lights were on everywhere, and Adey motioned towards the bathroom.

"He only used one paper towel, and he didn't get any blood on it."

Gamadge looked in. "That's the towel I used. Miss Bluett let me wash my hands in here."

"Wonder he didn't get you both. See what happened?" Adey turned slowly from left to right, shining his torch up the back stairs. "He was there. He listened in when you left and the Stapler boy left, went down cellar and got his maple log—if he didn't have it already. She was at her desk working. Coming in from the passage he'd get her from behind. If his shoes were tied up again, the way they were on Thursday night, she wouldn't hear a thing. Wouldn't *know* a thing—we hope."

"We hope."

Gamadge went along the passage and looked into the Library. It was dim, and Adey put all the lights on.

There was nobody at the desk now, but down on the floor, within the rampart of books, there was a huddle of cotton print and a great stain of blood. Books had toppled over; beneath them lay a section of maple wood, red where its end showed from among sprawling open volumes and white pages. Gamadge stood looking down, his eyes focused for the moment on a yellow pencil with a rubber stamp on it.

"Working all right," said Adey, following Gamadge's look. "Had her pencil in her hand. Ever see anything like it? I did: George Carrington." The silence lasted so long that he asked: "Make you feel funny or anything?"

"No, I'm all right. If he'd got me first, Adey—I was looking at these books—Miss Bluett would have screamed. The casements are open. He wouldn't have got away."

"That's so. But he don't mind risks—look at Thursday night. Crazy of course. Want to go upstairs?"

"If you don't mind."

"It's all right." Adey led the way. "Keep to the edges. He had newspapers all over the place up there, so we don't have to worry about the floors."

They went up to a little hall, from which doors opened.

"Used this one room," said Adey, "the one that faces the woods. He could show a light."

"Where do these newspapers come from?" Gamadge looked into the small room, cluttered with a carpet of old newsprint.

"Packing boxes in one of the other bedrooms. He must have had food with him, but perhaps he don't eat."

"Somebody mentioned bread crumbs."

"Just a grain or two, stale white bread."

Gamadge nodded and turned away. They went down two flights of stairs to the cellar, and Adey unbolted the door. Gamadge came out alone, and mounted the steps. A captain of state police stood talking to a man and a woman who faced him arm in arm. The man was Lawrence Carrington, the woman resembled him enough for Gamadge to think she must be Carrington's sister Lydia.

Lawrence had described her as serene, and Gamadge had received an impression from various persons that she was a spectator of life; her expressionless face was serene now as a mask is. But the arm within her brother's trembled slightly. She couldn't control that. Tall, pale-haired, beautifully dressed in white, she looked at Gamadge as if she did not see him.

The captain of state police was saying: "Just repeated himself, like they all do. You people here have had a raw deal, I don't say it's anybody's fault, but it was a raw deal. All safe now." He turned and saw Gamadge.

"Mr. Gamadge," murmured Carrington. "Captain White."

Captain White nodded, not too cordially, and went down the steps into the cellar.

Carrington said: "He's badly hit by this, never hear the end of it. Lydia?"

"Yes."

"This is Mr. Gamadge."

Her mouth formed a smile.

Gamadge said: "I wouldn't have thought of searching the Library myself on Thursday night."

"Nor I," agreed Carrington.

Lydia Carrington turned her head away. "Poor Hattie Bluett. I've known her all my life."

Gamadge said: "No reason for me to intrude myself on you tonight, Miss Carrington. All this is too much for you."

"Please come."

"We're counting on you more than ever. Do us good." Carrington looked around him at the crowd, and beyond it. "Where's Rose? Oh; talking to that young fellow— Yates. The fellow at the Wakefield Inn, Lydia." He pressed her arm gently. "You remember?"

"Yes, Mr. Yates," she repeated.

"He was the one that made Emmy Wakefield give the alarm on Thursday night."

"Yes."

"Or delayed her? Which? Never mind. Seven thirty, then, Gamadge. We won't wait for Rose, Lydia; I suppose that young man will see her safely home."

"Or I will," said Gamadge.

As they turned away, Gamadge went through the crowd to the place beyond it and beyond the library where Yates and Rose Jenner stood. They had the casual air towards each other of bystanders who have made acquaintance on the sidelines of some event or catastrophe. As he came up, Rose looked at Gamadge from brilliant half-closed eyes.

Yates stepped forward eagerly. "Gamadge—there don't have to be any secrets now?"

"No secrets now."

"Let me introduce you to Rose Jenner. Rose—our only friend." He was trying not to look too happy.

Gamadge said: "I don't seem to have done much for you."

"But we're grateful all the same." She did not smile, and Gamadge was also grave.

Yates said: "We're not going to tell the Carringtons that we knew each other before, though; don't forget, Gamadge, and give us away."

"Just one secret left after all?"

She said: "I don't want to hurt Lydia. Why should she know? I can bring Garry along this evening and they'll be glad to meet him. He's been a part of it—he's been through it all."

"We hope they'll ask me to stay for supper," said Yates, gaily in spite of himself.

"I'm sure they will," said Rose. Her voice was clear, pleasant, a little toneless; just the voice, Gamadge thought, which could be imagined pronouncing that small ancient doom: *Your king is in check*.

Yates could not help noticing Gamadge's gravity. He said: "This must be tough for you. Were you really with the poor Bluett woman just before?"

"Just before."

"It's pretty ghastly, isn't it, that her death should do so much for us? For the whole place, if it comes to that!"

"Well, not her death, exactly," replied Gamadge, and Rose Jenner's eyes opened wider. Gamadge could see the gold at the edge of the irises.

"Not her death?" Yates was taken aback.

"Well, no; not her death, but the fact that there are newspapers spread about upstairs in the Library."

Cars could be heard arriving at the foot of the path; people came up the path, carrying bags and cases. Yates said: "Let's move, Rose," and took hold of her elbow. One of the newcomers ran up to Gamadge and showed a badge. "Sheriff wants to know if you'll wait, Mr. Gamadge. I'm Rouse, deputy; saw you this morning."

"I remember. I *am* waiting."

Yates said: "Hope to see you at the Carringtons'." He and Rose moved off behind the Library. Gamadge settled down on the flat coping of an old stone wall, lighted a cigarette, and shut his eyes.

14. CLEARANCE

The deputy came out of the front door of the Library and lifted an arm. Gamadge rose and joined him. They went into the big book-lined room, where a small crowd was still busy in the corner behind Miss Bluett's desk. A bulb flashed.

The sheriff took Gamadge into a corner where hard library chairs were gathered as if for a conference. They sat down. Ridley had a cigar in his mouth, his hands on his knees. After a moment he said: "Guess it's all sewed up now."

"Except catching him."

"Yes. I'm waiting for that news. Lets you out, Mr. Gamadge."

"Lets some others out, doesn't it? For instance, everybody that had an alibi for this afternoon?"

"That's so. I wasn't worrying about them yet."

"But they're worrying, Sheriff."

"That's so. Feel like handing out the good news, do you?" Ridley got an envelope and a pencil out of his pocket. "Let's see."

"After all," continued Gamadge gently, "the maniac is still at large."

"My gosh, if we don't get him this time . . ."

"Some of those people will be glad to go."

"And I'll be glad to get rid of 'em. Those Silvers, for instance. They were all with Miss Wakefield and the Yates feller out back playing darts, Mrs. Silver and all. The boy got her to come down and play, said she was having nervous prostration up in her room and she had to come

134

down. Miss Wakefield and Yates have to stay, they're witnesses to the axe business Thursday night, they're needed at the inquest. The Silvers never saw a thing that night."

"And this afternoon clears young Silver."

"I'll send Rouse over, tell 'em they can pack up and go. Who else?"

"Some people at Edgewood. Motley and Mrs. Turnbull were talking to me on the side porch from the time I reached there after I left Miss Bluett. They were on the porch before that—Miss Pepper knows they were."

"And they're not witnesses either. They didn't see or hear anything Thursday night."

"No. I'm going back there; could I tell them? Could you give me a pass for them or something?"

The sheriff exchanged his pencil for a fountain pen, accepted a page of Gamadge's notebook, and wrote on it, the notebook for a pad.

"Write me two, will you, Sheriff?" Gamadge steadied the notebook. "Those people won't want to leave together, Mrs. Turnbull hasn't her car and she might not care to take a lift from Motley."

"That's so, strangers." The sheriff wrote two, and handed them over. Gamadge waved them until they were dry, then put them in his wallet.

"Haynes can't go," said Ridley. "Not on your life he can't. He was right there. By his own showing he was right up there behind the Library when the feller got away."

"Wouldn't have mentioned it, if he'd been the maniac, would he?"

"Don't know how crazy he might be. These crazy people are boastful—like to get as close to the spotlight as they can."

"Don't tell me, Sheriff, that you're forgetting those newspapers upstairs?"

"No, I'm not forgetting those newspapers upstairs. But I'm not letting Haynes go, and neither would you in my place. There's been enough mistakes made around here since Thursday night. I'm having folks warned to be more careful than they ever were. But it looks like the prowler now—unless he has some place here to hide, he's wandering in the woods. He's been smart, they often are, but he must be pretty crazy by this time. Well, we're having those newspapers analyzed, and the bread crumbs too; how's that?"

"That's sensible."

"I thought you'd laugh about the bread crumbs."

"No indeed."

"I did, but those state police technicians, they're just wild to get at those bread crumbs. Might be something in that bread that puts it in one bakery in the whole of Westchester county. They can't do much about the log of wood, though. Ever hear of that choice of weapon before? On the premises and doesn't take prints—maple bark doesn't anyway—and kills like a piece of iron. But what weapon did he bring along with him to the library? Of course there's a woodpile at Edgewood."

"Is there?"

"Right on his way. They've been cutting some hickory up there. We haven't found any lying around loose, though. He's got a wood complex."

"Evidently."

"So those technicians tell me. Took a look at that axe at Wakefield's and decided it wasn't what he wanted. I guess he must have brought along his own stick of wood, and liked the Carringtons' firewood and the firewood here better. You know, that rough bark—the blood didn't spatter much; but there must have been some on the killer; wouldn't you say so? Haynes—"

"Has Mr. Haynes got blood on him?"

"Plenty."

"Oh?"

"His own, from those scratches he picked up from the berry bushes on his way down from the wood path. We don't find any more yet."

"Are you going to lock Haynes up in a padded cell until

the technicians analyze his tweeds—or you find the real maniac?"

The sheriff took his cigar out of his mouth to smile. "What were you doing up on that stone wall back there? Asleep?"

"I was in a reverie, yes."

"You missed something. We had Haynes in here, looking him over, and that nurse—Pepper—pushed in and said he had heart trouble and we'd be responsible if we killed him, and that Miss Studley's patients were under Edgewood care, and that it was time for Hr. Haynes to come home and have his before-dinner sleep. She walked out of here with him, had hold of his arm; he went along with her, meek as a dog." The sheriff added: "So if you stay over you'll have the pleasure of being under the same roof with him. *Are* you staying over?"

"I am; I have a supper engagement at the Carringtons'."

The sheriff rose. "I'm going up there now; I have to talk over the inquest with Carrington, get his requests for the disposal of his father's body afterwards, lots of things."

Gamadge slowly got to his feet. "Then you can go home?"

"Home? I'll be here at the Tavern half the night; they might catch the murderer. Well, Mr. Gamadge, I'm mighty sorry you had your trip for nothing. Tell Durfee I was glad to make your acquaintance."

"I will, Sheriff." They shook hands.

Gamadge went down to the street, which was now lined with cars on both sides from one end of it to the other. He walked up the Edgewood drive. Edgewood had a dead and empty look, its front door closed and its windows shuttered against the setting sun. He rang, and Mrs. Norbury peeped at him through a crack. She flung the door wide.

"Well, young man! I don't know which is the hero of the hour—you or Haynes."

Gamadge entered. "Me?" he asked.

"Spending the afternoon in the Library with the murderer upstairs."

137

"Or down cellar."

"Poor thing, what a disagreeable girl she was."

"Just mannerism; they get it sometimes—that or claustrophobia."

"Got along with her, did you?"

"Very well indeed."

Mrs. Norbury surveyed him. "Now I look at you, you do show signs of having had a shock. Go up and get a pill from Miss Studley."

"That's an idea."

Gamadge ascended, but only to the second floor. He knocked on the door next his. After a pause Motley told him to come in.

Motley stood in his shirtsleeves, a water glass in his hand. The whiskey in the glass had not been diluted. He looked at Gamadge as if he hardly recognized him.

Gamadge held out one of the sheriff's passes. "Here you are. Beat it."

"What?"

"Beat it. Get in your car and go. Let them send your stuff after you. Say you've had a telephone call about a sick dog."

Motley took the slip of paper and read what was on it. A slow flush rose through the sickly yellow of his face. He looked at Gamadge, read the paper again, and said: "I thought I was a goner."

"Better get going, Motley."

"You got this for me?"

"You'd have had it sooner or later."

"A little too late." He put the whiskey tumbler down, half turned, stopped, and addressed Gamadge again; relief struggling in his expression with a queer resentment: "I wish I knew exactly who you are and what's in this for you."

"I'm thinking of Mrs. Turnbull."

Motley could not quite repress the beginnings of an incredulous leer. Knowing the kind of thing he would have liked to say and couldn't, Gamadge felt a little sorry for the fellow.

"Don't waste time over my motives," he said. "Think of it as a racket if you like. Only get out of this."

"I won't hit the village at all. I'll leave by way of Green Tree, drive straight for the river, cross by the Bear Mountain bridge, go home from there."

"That's right."

"I wish to God I knew why you thought of looking us up in the first place."

"I told you. Besides, you seemed so nervous. Don't try anything of the sort again, Motley, you're not equipped for it."

"Oh." Motley smiled. "Strings to this, are there?" He held up the pass. "I thought so."

"No strings, but of course I should follow your future career with interest."

"Especially if it gets mixed up with Mrs. Turnbull's?"

"Only if it gets into the papers."

Motley said almost violently: "You know the worst of me."

"I hope so."

Motley put the slip of paper in his wallet and picked up a small traveling case. Gamadge went out of the room, shutting the door after him, and back down the hall. He knocked at Mrs. Turnbull's door.

A faint voice asked who it was.

"Gamadge. May I come in a minute?"

The faint voice said yes. He went into a dim and perfumed retreat, and after a moment or so during which he got his bearings he saw Mrs. Turnbull. She was lying down on a bed which had certainly been furnished by herself with pink satin pillows and a pale, monogrammed eiderdown. This was spread over her feet. She lifted her head to gaze at him with red-rimmed eyes.

"It's all right, Mrs. Turnbull. May I give you this?" Gamadge came up to the bed and handed her the pass. "It lets you out of Frazer's Mills whenever you want to go."

Mrs. Turnbull reached feebly for her lorgnette; Gamadge put it into her hand. She scrutinized the pass.

"What I think is," said Gamadge, "that you'd better

139

wait on until the end of your booking. No reason at all why you should leave sooner; Motley's going immediately."

"Is he?"

"Of course. He's the one that makes it dangerous for both of you. I got one of those permissions for him, and he'll be out of here in half an hour."

"But will I be safe here?"

"Quite safe."

"Mrs. Norbury says that Mr. Haynes—"

"Don't worry about Mr. Haynes."

Mrs. Turnbull was incapable at the moment of being grateful for anything; indeed, she probably couldn't take in what she was to be grateful for. She said: "Well, if you say we're all right . . ."

"And you know what I think, Mrs. Turnbull? I think what you need is a nice long trip. Change, new friends, travel. Enjoy yourself. Meet new people."

"I don't make friends easily. I'm so *alone*."

"Well, you try it." He added, on a note of apology: "I suppose you have no financial affairs to worry about; I mean you're all tied up in a nice trust or something?"

"Oh, I'm tied up *tight*, Mr. Gamadge."

Feeling somewhat relieved, Gamadge went to his own room. At least Mrs. Turnbull wouldn't be murdered, whatever happened to her husbands; for she was fated. She was a predestined victim, and Gamadge was thankful that she would probably be the victim of nothing worse than a fortune hunter.

It was time for him to get ready for supper at the Carringtons'. He had a bath, dressed at leisure, and was downstairs at twenty past seven. On his way to the telephone he met Miss Pepper.

"When you write to your husband," he said, "tell him that an obscure civilian named Gamadge is proud of you."

"Miss Studley's furious at them. Poor Mr. Haynes. But he didn't have an attack, blue as he looked. If they dare bother him again—"

"Do excuse me, won't you, I have to telephone my wife. Haven't had time all day."

Gamadge went back to the booth. Several minutes later he came out of it looking as if his time there had not been ill-spent. He left Edgewood at a fast walk, and kept up the pace when he reached the street; but he crossed to the other side to avoid the worst of the crowd.

The Library was now dark, and there were few people gazing at it from the lawn. Gamadge wondered who would sit at Miss Bluett's desk now, or if anybody would. Probably it would never function as a library again, but would go into the market as a desirable all-the-year-round residence and bring taxpayers and new blood to Frazer's Mills.

In front of the Wakefield Inn young Silver was tinkering with a sedan. He left his job when he caught sight of Gamadge, and ran across to speak to him.

"Isn't this rotten?"

"About Miss Bluett? Yes. Rotten."

"Well, of course that's terrible; but I mean isn't it rotten we're going?"

"Don't you want to go?"

"Certainly I don't. Not with all the excitement, and besides that we have no place to go to but my aunt's, and I have to sleep three in a room with my cousins. Worst little aggregation of dim thinkers you ever saw. When I got the news of course I came and told the parents, and they started packing; my father has a logical mind, he knew they'd let us go. He's been pestering them ever since. We're leaving now."

"Well, I'm very glad to have met you, Mr. Silver."

"No, but they say you're a friend of the sheriff's or something; they say the cops passed you right in, you must have something to do with the law."

"Grapevine still working, I see. I have no official connection with the law. I happen to know some people—"

"Listen, Mr. Gamadge. If I had evidence they'd make me stay. The family could go, but I could stay till after the inquest. I'd have to."

"What do you mean, evidence?"

"Well, listen; you know where my sleeping porch is, and I was reading there on Thursday night—had my light on. Well, this maniac must have gone round the house from north to south on his way to Carringtons'. He'd see my light when he got round, and he'd cut back up to the wood path; wouldn't he?"

"Very likely."

"That's what he did do. I've been pretty sure of it ever since, but the parents said I wasn't sure enough to make my evidence worth talking about."

"I don't know what *you* are talking about."

"Well, looking back after all the hullabaloo, I was pretty sure I heard him going up through the orchard to the wood path. Anyway, I heard something. Isn't that evidence?"

"If it is, and you've concealed it until now, they'll make it hot for you; minor though you are. They'll make it hot for your father and mother."

"Not if we say we weren't sure."

"We? We?"

"The parents kept insisting that I imagined it afterwards, or that it was a bird or an animal."

"Put it on them, would you?"

"No, but you know they'd mix in."

"Then you keep them out. You can't swear to anything, and this evidence isn't needed now. Everybody knows the maniac must have gone past the Inn, and you'll have to go and sleep three in a room with your backward cousins."

Young Silver resigned himself. "I can't find Yates anywhere," he said, turning away. "Will you say goodbye for me?"

"Yes. It really was a pleasure to meet you, Mr. Silver."

"Thanks."

He went back to the family car. Gamadge walked on past Wakefield and Carrington property, and crossed when he was opposite the Carringtons' picket gate. He went through the gate, and up a flagged walk darkly shadowed by pines.

15. THE TRELLIS

Gamadge stood at the foot of the broad and shallow steps that led up to the porch, and looked to right and left. On the left the grounds were rough and thickly planted with trees; on the right the side lawn, landscaped in its old-fashioned way with round flowerbeds and towerlike trellis, sloped green and picturesque to barns and stables. In this half light it was charming; Gamadge thought how pleasant it must be of a summer morning, with all its fragrance of honeysuckle vine and flowers, damp earth and new-cut grass.

There was a bow window on this side of the house, and below it, running all along the foundations, a deep moat or ditch, fern-planted, gave light to basement windows. Farther along there was another bow. Gamadge had walked to the corner to observe all this; now he came back, mounted the steps, and rang a bell that tinkled softly.

Carrington opened the door; he was in dinner clothes.

"I'm sorry," said Gamadge, "I didn't bring other garments."

"Stupid of me not to realize that—or at least to ask. Not that it matters. My father," said Carrington, "liked us to dress. He never relaxed in such ways, not even at The Mills. It's automatic with us now. Do come in. The cocktails are ready."

He led the way into a parlor on the right, from which two doorless archways gave on an inner room. They, as well as the front windows and the bow, were corniced in gilt and draped with cherry brocade much faded.

"What a room," said Gamadge, while Carrington went to a console to pour the cocktails.

"Too bad Lydia can't face it yet. You know that"— he moved his head slightly—"is where my father was killed."

"I supposed so."

"And Lydia's piano is here. Too bad. Well, they say times cures everything if we wait."

The room, smelling sweetly of old painted wood, old fires, straw matting and many flowers, was all white, cherry brocade and rosewood. Gamadge, his cocktail glass in hand, wandered about looking at pictures and ornaments. The flowers were in trumpet-shaped glass vases with ormolu holders and stands. "Lovely," said Gamadge.

"Rose arranges them," said Carrington. "Extraordinary how much of our old stuff has survived. We have never replaced anything." He added: "We'll be getting electric light now; my father preferred the oil lamps and the candles, but it's really too difficult to get regular service, and lamps have to be filled and wicks trimmed if the skies fall. And fires built." He looked down at the hearth. "You see where the log was."

The top log was in fact missing from the well-laid pile. Gamadge nodded.

"Shall we go into the bedroom now, and have our second drink afterwards?" Carrington stood aside, and Gamadge went past him into an oblong room, wider than it was deep. The big four-poster bed faced the wall between the doorways; glazed chintz curtained it, but the curtain to the left of the headboard was missing.

There were two rear windows, looking out on greenery; there was a bow window looking out on the side lawn. Rosewood furniture, very handsome; old hooked rugs in fine condition; a marble-topped night table furnished with a lamp and candles, writing materials, books.

"You can see," said Carrington, "that in warm weather this would be the most comfortable room in the house. My father always had it, and his father before him. Upstairs the ceilings are lower, and no room but this has nearly the amount of air. With the front door open, as it was on Thursday, as he always wanted it to be until late, he got all the air there was on a hot night. It can be hot in Frazer's Mills. But not too hot, you know." He smiled.

"Never too hot if you like a place," said Gamadge.

"Place is like a garden in summer," said Carrington. "And it's as it always was, except that my father very reluctantly parted with the old washstand and painted tin ewers and things when he put in his ground-floor bathroom. That's our one innovation, and most convenient. I believe we had the first bathtub ever seen in Frazer's Mills—but that was long ago. A coffin-shaped tin affair, and cold water piped upstairs. The wonders of science."

"You got ahead of the Chapleys and Compsons and the rest of them?"

"They were all taking cat-washes in tin basins while my great-grandfather luxuriated in his coffin, like Donne."

Gamadge's eyes traveled about the room. The silver on the bureau top was so old that its engraved monograms were all but effaced; beautiful stuff. Everything of a personal kind was rich and beautiful, from the thick silk of the dark dressing-gown that hung on a chair back to the squares of writing paper in a lacquered case on the night stand.

Gamadge went up to look at it. "I love such paper."

"Part of my father's pre-war stock; he always got it from England, and it had to be that shade of off-white. If it came gray, or café-au-lait, or white, you know, back it went."

"I sympathize. Nothing like the right thing." Gamadge fingered a corner of the paper lovingly, and admired the spidery and ornate monogram.

"There's that book," said Carrington, "that didn't get sent to the Library."

Gamadge picked the thin volume up from the night table. "Oh yes; Miss Bluett told me about it, poor soul, while I was with her this afternoon; I wonder if her murderer profited by our literary conversation."

Carrington drew his shoulders together and exhaled a

breath. Then, as Gamadge turned pages, he came and looked over his shoulder. "How fond we were of that set. We always had it out on rainy days when we were children. *The Woodpecker, The Thrush, The Starling.* Nicely colored, aren't they?"

"They are."

"A regional book; Mrs. E. Lampton was a Westchester woman, and a sentimental one. Her prose errs on the side of poesy. Too bad we got the set into such poor condition."

"I'm thinking what nice paper they made in those days for such books, and what nice paper the British make still. Look." He drew out a protruding leaf, and held it beside the writing paper in the lacquer case. "Rag paper, quarto size, and this is discolored to your father's favorite shade of off-white. You'd hardly know the difference to sight or touch, would you?"

Carrington looked from one specimen to the other, looked closer, then smiled. "Well, you're an expert; I suppose this is the kind of things you notice in your professional work?"

"And in my extra-professional work."

"All that kind of information—or observation, trained observation, must come in very handy."

"It does. As you say," and Gamadge replaced the leaf in the bird book, "too bad the set is in such poor condition."

"That's what my father said when he saw them—the first time, I do believe, since he was a child on a rainy day himself. They were in the attic, have been ever since they ceased to be presentable. He wanted a last look at the woodpecker and the starling before they went away forever. So like Hattie Bluett to send over at seven o'clock and demand them and the rest of the lot—salt of the earth, but she did love ordering us about when she could. And so like her to decide to put labels in all the poor old books on Thursday night if it killed her. She was going off on that awful jaunt of hers the next day; a bus trip to Boston, I think, and there's some hotel that has arrangements for a whole party to pig together in one room; five double-decker beds in it."

"Cosy."

"Well, she sent Hawkins for the books. Hattie Bluett always rather intimidated Lydia, so poor Lydia came in here and collected the birds. If I'd been on hand or known anything about it Hawkins would have been sent empty away. My father was asleep; Lydia hurried over the job, and what with her hurry and her efforts to make no noise, that volume got left behind. The others were on a chair beside the bed. He must have been reading the one you have, and set it down. In fact he was reading something when I was here, just before his tray came in. I took the tray from Mrs. Begbie; I think I remember that he was reading, and did set the book aside. Then I went up to change. I never saw him alive again."

"He went to sleep soon after he'd had his supper, then?"

"Just tea and toast, something very light. Afterwards he'd take his ten grains of aspirin; and what with his slight fever and the aspirin he'd soon drop off." Carrington went over to the bow window and stood there in the failing light, looking out. "I'm afraid he sounds neglected."

"No. Why?"

"People always say so when there's been a tragedy. But Rose dashed off right after dinner to her movie, and I was in the library, and after Lydia looked in here at nine she went upstairs herself. She wanted him to sleep —she didn't even light the lamps in her sitting room across the hall. He could get about, you know; took care of himself, loathed nursing. I'd been trying to get him to let Miss Studley or the other nurse come down and give him heat therapy; he wouldn't hear of it. A call from him—from the hall—would have brought both of us on the run."

"I know, Carrington. I know."

"That damned front door. But it was always his own wish in hot weather, and we're used—we were used to thinking of Frazer's Mills as our own front yard." Carrington turned. "I suppose the Library will close up now —none too soon. The books will go at auction. Or are they even worth a sale, I wonder?"

Gamadge said: "I might take this over and put it with the rest, if you like."

"When?"

"Tonight. I thought I'd like to pay the Library another visit before I left. I'm off tomorrow."

Carrington looked surprised. "Another visit? Why?"

"I didn't half see it this afternoon. There are one or two things I'd like to see again." Gamadge added: "Without publicity."

"Have you a key?"

"No; I thought perhaps Hawkins—"

"Hawkins, or one of the state police might have his. I'll telephone for you. Go with you, if you like—you might care to see what the back way and the wood path are like at night."

"It's exactly what I *would* like."

"We'll go then, after dinner. Bring that thing along, will you?"

Gamadge, the bird book in hand, followed Carrington back into the parlor. Carrington, at the cocktail tray, said: "Must leave enough for the young people—Lydia won't touch gin. She'll have a sherry. Oh, by the way, I didn't tell you; Rose has acquired a young man. He's staying for supper."

"Good."

"That Yates fellow who had a call from the murderer at the Wakefield Inn, and had fortunately locked his door. But you know all that. Rose met him this afternoon. I think she has some vague idea that he's a fellow sufferer; I don't know why, unless it's because he'll be a witness at the inquest. Lydia and I feel that Rose is a sufferer, and we were glad to give her young company since she wants it. Young people get acquainted rapidly nowadays." He poured drinks.

Gamadge, sipping his, said that Yates seemed a pleasant youth.

"Thank heaven she's found somebody at last whom we can like. You've no idea, Gamadge, what oddities she managed to pick up in New York. My father—well, in this case you couldn't have called him too fastidious. There was a married man, at least forty years old, a European, I don't know exactly from where. His reminiscences were interminable. Then there was a youngish individual who needed a shave and a clean collar, and who didn't rise when my sister came into the room. Rose said he was very interesting. Another lout, on leave from the army, lectured us on the post-war world; and at that time we weren't even living in it. Well, Rose had had a curious life, in some ways she's old for her age. I dare say she did find these people intellectually stimulating— more so than the upper bourgeoisie whom we offered her. Now, however, she's back to normal with Mr. Yates. Thank heaven."

Gamadge said that Yates seemed a normal type enough.

"Just the thing for Rose. I hope he has prospects. She has none, poor child, one of the minor tragedies connected with my father's death. If he'd lived, and she hadn't married, I'm sure he would have arranged life insurance for her benefit. As it is—"

Footsteps sounded on the porch. Carrington put down his glass and went to open the door. When he returned, Rose Jenner and Yates followed him; she had changed into a long dress, yellow with white flowers. She nodded to Gamadge, took her cocktail and went across the room to the bow window. Standing there and looking out, her dark hair loose on her neck, she was an exotic figure in that formal setting, where the very richness of ornament looked prim.

Yates, standing with his back to her at the console, between the other men, said under his breath: "She's terribly upset by this Bluett thing."

"Is she? Well, I suppose so." Carrington poured his drink. "We all are."

"But she's—she seems to feel it more and more."

"Frightened of the tramp?"

"It may be that."

"Perhaps it's more personal. She read a good deal in the Library. She may have made friends with Miss Bluett."

Gamadge shook his head. "I don't think so. Miss Bluett mentioned her to me, but only as a reader."

"What she can have found there to read!"

"Oh, lots of things." Gamadge smiled. "That's why I borrowed Miss Bluett's key—to read there. But I handed it back to the authorities."

"Hattie Bluett lent you her key?" Carrington was astonished and amused. "You must have the tongue of angels."

"No, merely a lot of useless information."

"I don't think many people of your kind—if there are many—bothered to talk to poor Hattie."

Rose Jenner suddenly turned; she said in a strained, hurried way, as if she had come to a decision once for all: "He could have hidden in the trellis."

The three men stared.

"There's a broken part on the other side," she went on quickly. "I saw it early this summer, when I was looking at the honeysuckle. Just now I—he could be there this moment, and nobody would know."

Carrington exclaimed: "You must be off your head," and strode across the room to the bay. The others followed him. All three windows were up; Yates leaned from the middle one where Rose had stood; Gamadge from the one on the right. Carrington from the third.

The trellis, not fifteen yards away, rose four-sided and tapering, shrouded in its vines. From the north it simply presented a leafy wall of green.

Carrington withdrew his head. "Perfectly ridiculous. How would a prowler know that he could get into the thing? Nobody's ever been inside of it since it was constructed—who'd get such an idea? How should anybody of that kind even *think* of it?"

Rose said: "I just had the idea."

"Well, it isn't a cheerful one." Yates looked down at her, smiling. "Want me to settle it, Miss Jenner? Here and now?"

Carrington answered him: "Better lay that ghost on the spot . . . Very good of you, Yates." He added, eyeing Yates whimsically behind Rose's back: "Will you have a weapon of some kind? How about a walking stick? My —there's a blackthorn in the hall stand."

Yates said he didn't think he'd bother with the blackthorn; he went out, and presently they heard his steps on the porch. Then they all saw him come around the corner of the house and walk towards the trellis over the short grass.

Carrington said: "Really, my dear child, a fatuous idea."

"You'd have said so if I'd asked if he might be in the Library."

"Right as usual; but a trellis . . . !"

Yates turned and waved to them. He went around to the far side of the trellis, and was lost to view. The three, leaning from the windows of the bay, waited.

Twilight had fallen. The trees and bushes of the lawn were motionless in the sad quiet of the late summer evening. Carrington said: "He'll come out covered with spiders' webs and old birds' nests."

Yates came around the trellis, stopped, and looked up at them. There was an odd expression on his face, a mixture of incredulity and astonishment. In his hand he held a piece of wood, a two-foot section of oak like a club. He said: "Nothing there but this."

Rose Jenner, her elbows on the sill, did not move. Gamadge, eyes fixed on the cudgel, was silent. Carrington, after a pause of stupefaction, shouted: "You found that thing in there?"

"Yes, in among a lot of weeds."

Gamadge withdrew his head to meet Carrington's amazed eyes. Carrington said almost in a whisper: "That weapon they thought he must have carried with him— but why should he think of putting it into the trellis?"

Rose said: "They say he had a flashlight."

"They think he had." Carrington gazed at her profile. "What on earth gave you the notion?"

"I don't know."

Yates called up to them: "Shall I bring it in?"

"For God's sake," Carrington told him, leaning out again, "don't let Lydia see it. Put it back. I suppose you ought never to have moved it."

"It wouldn't take prints."

"No, but they'll want to see where it was, and how long it's been there."

"I can put it where it was." Yates looked at it. "It's old wood. Picked up somewhere and broken off short. I'm awfully sorry if I've done the wrong thing, Mr. Carrington."

"Doesn't matter, I'm sure."

"I was so staggered when I made it out by the light of a match, down among the dandelions and the chickweed."

"Well, put it back; or—want to look at it, Gamadge?"

Gamadge shook his head.

Yates went around the trellis. He returned, crossed the lawn at a fast pace, and came back into the house. The others met him as he entered.

"Well!" he said, looking from Rose to Carrington. "So that's what he—"

"We don't know, of course." Carrington was frowning. "Might be something Begbie pushed into the place for some reason or no reason. To get rid of it. He'll never say so if he thinks it's important. They never do. What I do not understand is Rose's inspiration. Uncanny." He looked at her with knitted brows.

"The whole thing's been so on her mind," said Yates, and Gamadge wondered how long he would be able to keep up a pretense of recent acquaintanceship.

"Of course," Carrington turned his puzzled face to Gamadge, "the man himself was never there. That's—"

"Doesn't look as if he had been," said Yates. "The weeds aren't crushed down, and there doesn't seem to be

152

any fresh break in the trellis. There'd hardly be room for him to crawl through without smashing crosspieces. Those breaks are old. The thing's pretty rotten-looking, Mr. Carrington."

"I dare say. I'll speak to Begbie about repairs this fall. And now, hang it all"—Carrington looked from Gamadge to Yates—"I suppose we'll have to have the whole lot of them crawling over the place again. Rotten? The whole trellis will be down. More publicity. Well, can't be helped, I suppose."

"It wouldn't do to keep it to ourselves, would it?" Rose spoke without much interest.

"Well, no. No. I hardly like to suppress it. Let them make what they can of the thing. We'll even admit we moved it, because if we deny it they'll know we're lying." He smiled faintly. "They know people do move things— we're not robots, much as they wish we were, sometimes. But remember, now; Lydia isn't to hear a word. If she must, she must—later; not yet. She's had enough."

Rose said: "Lydia ought to know."

He swung to look at her. "Why?"

"It'll simply frighten her to have people here again and not know why."

"I'll tell her then; tonight."

Gamadge said: "We can tell the authorities when we ask for the key."

"So we can."

Rose asked: "Key?" but just then Lydia Carrington came to the door. She said: "Supper's ready." Her white dress gave her a yellow look; it wasn't the right shade of white for her faded blondness.

"And much help we've been to you," said Carrington.

"There was hardly anything to do; Mrs. Begbie left everything ready."

Rose said: "I'm sorry, Lydia."

"My dear child! I'm glad you had a little pleasure. It was high time."

They all went out into the hall and back to the dining

room; Carrington last. The front door was closed, and Carrington waited to pull down a lamp on a ceiling chain and light the wick. It spread a pale, mellow glow, just right for the pale old woodwork and engravings of the wide hall.

16. OBSESSION

Candles burned on the long table in the dining room, on the white chimney piece and in wall brackets. The buffet held platters of cold chicken and ham, salad, fruit; there was a huge silver coffee urn.

People helped themselves and sat down. Gamadge found himself beside Rose Jenner. He said: "I understand that you're a chess player, Miss Jenner."

"I play. I'm not really good. I was as good when I was ten years old as I ever will be; my father taught me all the gambits, that's all."

"All? If the gambits were all! But there comes the awful moment for duffers when the other fellow refuses to respond any longer; what then? Then people like you exercise your strange power of knowing what people like me will do long before we know it ourselves."

"I could never win against a real master."

"Have you tried?"

"No, and I never shall."

"You'd play an amateur, though?"

"I hope I'll never have to look at a board again. Thank goodness Garry doesn't know a knight from a queen." She spoke low.

"Oh, everybody knows a knight from a queen. Let's say he wouldn't know that the game was lost until the final move."

Yates, sitting beyond her, had been talking to Lydia Carrington. He turned. "Let's forget chess," he said. "Let's stick to the great outdoors. What do you say, Miss

Jenner? How about a drive after supper? Take in Westbury night life."

Carrington, circulating with a bottle of white wine, said that that would be a good idea.

"If it's safe." Lydia, hardly touching her food, had sat silent. Now, with a suddenness that startled them all, she half rose from the table; her low voice changed into an unrecognizable strained cry: "Did anybody lock the front door?"

They sat in consternation, looking at her—Gamadge, Rose Jenner and Yates. Carrington, wine bottle in hand, stood behind Gamadge's chair, his hand on the back of it; the shock of his sister's wild question had so staggered him for the moment that he clung to the curved wood as if for support.

She gasped: "I'm sorry. I can't help it. Since Thursday I can't think of anything else."

Yates got up. "I'll see, Miss Carrington."

Lawrence said: "I'm pretty sure I locked it before I lighted the hall lamp. I could almost swear—wait, I'll go."

"If you didn't, Lawrence," said Lydia, faintly, "we must search the whole house; we must look in the pediment again." She stood leaning forward, both hands on the table; looking at no one, she waited in that position until Carrington had gone out through the sitting room and returned.

"Locked," he said.

Then she sat slowly down. "I'm awfully sorry. It's an obsession, I know."

"*We* aren't blaming you, Lydia," said Rose.

Anything more curiously out of character than Lydia's outburst, and the tone and manner of it, Gamadge had never seen or heard. She had been a different person; that was what had startled them all, including her brother, so much. Now Carrington poured wine into her glass and patted her shoulder.

"Blame you? No! You're absolutely right." He came back to his place beside Gamadge. "I simply can't tell her," he muttered, "about that stick in the trellis. Thing to do is to get her mind off. She goes over and over that night, but my father was dead long before Emeline called me."

"These things don't go by logic."

"If she can just begin to think of something else. That damned inquest. I wonder if they'd let her off." He looked at Gamadge, anxious and worried. "Would they? On my report? She won't see a doctor."

"A statement from her ought to do." Gamadge tasted his wine. What a connoisseur George Carrington had been. Miss Carrington, at the other end of the table, was drinking hers. Color had begun to rise in her face—its deathly pallor was gone.

Rose asked: "What was that key you were talking about, Lawrence?"

"Key?"

"You said something to Mr. Gamadge about a key— just before we came in to supper."

"Trust you, Rosie, not to forget anything." He smiled. "Gamadge and I are going to take a walk to the Library."

Lydia turned her eyes to Gamadge. "Why?"

"Mr. Gamadge wants to go, for some mysterious reason." He added: "We shan't leave you alone. Whoever brings the key will stay here with you until we get back —if Rose and Mr. Yates are off on their drive."

"I can wait. We can wait," said Rose.

"Of course," said Yates.

"No need of that. I don't mind being alone," said Lydia. "I don't mind at all. But I don't like all this wandering around."

"*Let us have no meandering,*" quoted Lawrence, smiling at her. "You wouldn't box us up forever, would you?"

"They've probably caught the tramp already," said Yates.

"We'd have heard."

Lydia said: "I don't need a policeman."

"But I need one to guard the house." Carrington drank the last of his coffee and went back into the library. They heard him telephoning. Everybody got up; Rose, Yates and Gamadge, over Lydia's protests, cleared the table and buffet and stacked dishes in the pantry. Lydia and Rose went to the kitchen, Yates and Gamadge handed dishes through the slide and received them and the silver back for drying.

Yates, after a silence during which Gamadge hummed maddeningly, spoke at last: "That was damn funny, wasn't it, Rose thinking about the trellis and me finding that stick there?"

"Miss Jenner, Miss Jenner. Don't forget your part, you know."

"I will, sooner or later. It would be better to come out with the whole thing; I'm going to tell Rose so. These Carringtons are decent sensible people, not hipped and prejudiced like the old man."

"What a way to talk about the deceased."

"I don't know what's the matter with you. Usually you're the life of the party."

"Chase yourself. My worst enemy never called me that."

"I mean you don't talk."

"This is a house of mourning. We've been eating funeral baked meats, my boy. Vivacity, even from a conversationalist like me, wouldn't do."

"I think it was very strange of Rose to think of that trellis. Almost like second sight," persisted Yates doggedly.

"What do you want me to do? Contradict you? Say that it wasn't strange at all, say that it was quite natural in the circumstances for her to think of it? Or do you want me to say that she probably looked into the trellis earlier, and saw the stick, and only decided to mention it because there's been a second murder and newspapers on the second floor of the Library?"

"Gamadge—"

"It was always good evidence that there was a prowler, you know. I mean it always would have been good evidence to that effect."

"I think it was almost second sight."

"A wife with second sight; interesting. Look out, don't bang that copper lustre down like that, it's survived a couple of centuries without being nicked."

"No orders from you," muttered Yates.

"Then don't annoy me by asking questions you don't want answered."

"I want to know how Rose knew there was a stick in the trellis," said Yates desperately.

"Ask her, and if she won't answer, ask no more."

Carrington put his head in. "It's all right, that nice fellow Adey is bringing Hawkins' key. No news. Will you come out with me, Gamadge, while I show him that stick? Less fuss the better."

On their way through the dining room to the library Gamadge asked: "Is Adey coming over immediately?"

"Well, no. He said a quarter of an hour. But I thought we might have a few minutes' quiet talk, and a cigar and a spot of brandy."

"And a spot of privacy, perhaps." Gamadge looked around the library with admiration. "What a perfect room. What a perfect house."

"This used to be called the study in olden days; they were more sensible of values then." Carrington closed folding doors that shut them off from the dining room. "That means a business conference," he said, "and no Carrington woman has ever allowed a business conference to be disturbed by anything short of a fire or a death. Birth, no; decidedly not."

Gamadge declined a cigar. Carrington went to a wall cupboard and got out a decanter and small glasses.

"And a business conference," he went on, filling the glasses, "was nine times out of ten a horse trade. Those horses. I was brought up on them. So was Lydia. We can recite a list of winners that would astonish you." He handed Gamadge a glass, and they sat down with a little table between them. Carrington lighted his cigar. "Bay Leaf, Bay Tree, Bay Rum, Bayberry, Bay Belle, Bay Billy—want me to go on?"

Gamadge laughed and said he was sufficiently impressed.

"And I'll give you a thousand guesses," said Carrington, "what our village anthem was—our song of triumph."

"I'll take one guess . . . *Camptown Races*—slightly adapted?"

"Somebody bet on the bay, all right! . . . You wanted to say something particular, Gamadge?" Carrington looked at him, his face again serious.

"Yes. I don't usually offer this kind of suggestion, Carrington, but I'm not at all sure that I advise mentioning that stick in the trellis to Adey—at least not until I've had another look round in the Library—the Rigby Library."

Carrington, surprised, studied him. "Why not?"

"Well—I suppose the whole thing still strikes you as very remarkable—Miss Jenner's inspiration?"

Carrington, his eyes on Gamadge's, frowned. "Yes, of course it does."

"Even Yates, who seems to be greatly taken with Miss Jenner, boggles at it; he's trying to ascribe it to second sight."

"To tell you the truth, it looked like that to me. Not that I believe in second sight. But—"

"It was strange, Carrington. Wouldn't Ridley and the state police ask themselves whether it wasn't too strange? Wouldn't they ask themselves whether she didn't *know* that cudgel was there?"

"But why—"

Gamadge leaned back and crossed one foot over the other knee. He clasped the ankle in a strong grip, as if to keep the foot from moving. "This is strictly between ourselves, for the time being. Not for the world would I mention it to anyone else—until I've had another look at the Library."

"But why the Library, Gamadge?"

"I don't think I'll find evidence there. But if I could . . . Carrington, has it occurred to you that those newspapers and bread crumbs and what-not might be a plant?"

"A—" Carrington looked stunned.

"It's assumed that because Miss Bluett was locked in, this afternoon, nobody could murder her who wasn't already there. But suppose somebody she knew came and reached up and tapped on a casement window—and called to her? She'd let that person in."

Carrington, sitting forward in his chair, shook his head as if to shake off the idea. "You're not thinking of Rose? Rose Jenner? What possible motive—"

"The prosecution," said Gamadge, "doesn't have to find motive if there's evidence. Let's look at what evidence there is—what evidence the police might find if they followed my train of reasoning."

"There's none—unless you mean her idea about that stick in the trellis."

"May it have been put there because I made the faintest possible suggestion to Miss Jenner, after the Bluett murder, that those newspapers in the Rigby Library can have been a plant?"

"To—you mean to—"

"To reinforce the prowler theory."

Carrington sat back. "I don't believe it!"

"I'm not asking you to believe it, I'm asking you to consider it from the police point of view. From my point of view, if you like, because I have information they wouldn't get except through me. For instance: Miss Bluett told me that Miss Jenner browsed in the Library; there's a shelf of criminology there, and one of the books—a book young Silver had—deals with exactly the kind of homicidal maniac we're supposed to have had in Frazer's Mills. That's thin enough, but it at least shows that Rose Jenner had access to a report on procedure."

Carrington's cigar had gone out. He lighted it again with fingers that were not too steady. "Vaguest kind of conjecture," he said around the cigar.

"It piles up into something. Why if there was no prowler, should anybody kill Miss Bluett? Because she was librarian at the Rigby Library? Because she might have supplied evidence against Rose Jenner if she'd been called upon to do so? She'd know more than anyone about Rose Jenner's reading. The classic motive there would be blackmail, but I don't see Miss Hattie Bluett in the part."

"As a blackmailer? No! Morally incredible."

"I agree with you. Does anyone know exactly where Rose Jenner was at those times this afternoon?"

"I suppose not. But—"

"Mightn't she have had a chance—while she was supposed to be changing for dinner, say, and Yates was elsewhere—"

"He was in here with me."

"Mightn't she have left the house by a back door and picked up that oak cudgel at the edge of the woods?"

"There are oaks everywhere." Carrington paused. "You're implying that those other visits on Thursday night—to Edgewood and the Wakefield Inn—were camouflage."

"Yes. I'm stating it."

"And that her objectives were Hattie Bluett and my father. Gamadge, she was fond of my father."

Gamadge uncrossed his foot from the other knee, leaned forward, and picked up his brandy. He half emptied the tiny glass, put it down, and sat back in his chair. "Let's talk about *her* father. How erratic was he?"

"Erratic is putting it mildly."

"She may have inherited a certain instability?"

Carrington, very reluctantly, said that Rose Jenner was impulsive; he and Lydia had put it down to youth and her bringing-up.

"The chess couldn't have been good for her nerves? Iron discipline, mental discipline, and then reaction from it?"

"Perhaps so. Nothing that could possibly make us think she oughtn't to marry, Gamadge."

"But is it barely possible that your father knew more about her background and parentage than you did? If he wanted to be of help to her, for his daughter's sake, he wouldn't tell all he knew. May he have discouraged her friendships with men for some such reason as I suggest?"

"I never thought of it. My God, Lydia mustn't hear any of this."

"What if Rose Jenner had developed persecution mania, with a real grudge behind it? Your father could not only have prevented her marriage for a year or so, he might—if he had this special knowledge—have prevented it forever."

Carrington said after a silence: "If it were a question of some sudden uncontrollable impulse, I might be able to entertain the idea. But my father's death didn't result from somebody's attack of acute mania."

"No, quite a different thing."

"This is ghastly. Even if it were true, which I don't for one moment admit, it might be something that would never recur. Marriage—happiness. Gamadge—you haven't spoken to the police yet; you said this was to be between us."

"I shouldn't dream of speaking to the police on what I have."

"But even if you did find something more—I can't imagine what it could be—is there any hope, any hope whatever, that you still wouldn't use your knowledge? You've told me this to warn me. I ought to be grateful, I am grateful. Well, I'm warned, and I give you my word that I won't let the thing end here. I'll speak to Lydia, we'll arrange something—alienists. I give you my word."

"So long as you *are* warned—"

"I give you my word. Let me be frank—I never liked her much; too alien, and there were selfish reasons: she upset our little unimportant routine. But I assure you I don't believe that she had this in her. Lydia will—she'll be infuriated at the notion."

Gamadge said: "I think Miss Carrington has worked it out for herself."

"You *do?*"

Gamadge looked steadily at him. "Didn't that outburst of hers at supper strike you as far from normal?"

"But I told you—an obsession." Carrington stared at him.

"I didn't express myself accurately. Didn't it strike you as artificial?"

Carrington turned very white; he seemed to shrink away from Gamadge, unable to speak.

"As if," said Gamadge, "*she* were trying to emphasize the existence of the prowler."

"Gamadge . . . Don't. . . ."

"Just so you're warned." Gamadge had picked up his brandy glass. Looking down at it, he repeated in a low voice: "Just so you're warned."

The doorbell tinkled. Carrington sprang up and went to the folding doors; rolling them wide, he said in a different, casual tone: "I see Lydia's in her sitting room. Will you go through, while I let Adey in?"

Gamadge went through, and found Lydia knitting in a pleasant room opposite the parlor. She looked up to give him an odd, strained smile.

"Rose and Mr. Yates slipped away. What a very nice young man he is, Mr. Gamadge; but what easy manners these children have. First names on short acquaintance. Do you like all that?"

"My tastes are prehistoric."

"I'm so glad. I often wondered whether our family were the only survivors."

Officer Adey appeared in the doorway, his sun-burned cheeks crimson in the lamplight. He had obviously been told to cheer Miss Carrington up.

"Well, *Ma'am*," he said breezily. "I guess you must be sick of the sight of us fellers. So if you like I'll sit out in the hall."

"Certainly not; I have coffee for you."

"That's fine, but do you know what I'd like when these people go? I'd like to see the pictures of those horses from way back."

"Would you really, Officer?"

"I always heard about those pictures. I want to see that one of Bay Belle. Ran against Maud S., didn't she?"

164

"And came back in disgrace."

"No singin' that night in Frazer's Mills! That was the life, race night, and everybody tight in the Tavern. How did they change the song? Let's see . . ."

"Don't put money on—"

"The bobtail nag. That's right."

"You sound as though you belonged, Officer Adey."

"I am, my great-grandpop was a trainer."

"No! Whose?"

"Compsons'."

Lydia got up. "The pictures are in a special bin in the library. Water colors and all."

They disappeared into the dining room. Carrington entered, the bird book in his hand. He said: "All right, Gamadge, I have a torch for you. Let's go."

17. EVIDENCE

They went along the hall to the back door; Carrington stopped to open a cupboard beside it and take down a rifle.

"Adey says the fellow must have sunk into the ground." He spoke with his back to Gamadge. "Might as well bring the Winchester along, I suppose." He turned. "Have you a gun?"

"Yes."

"Good. It's a dark walk—if you still want to take it? You wouldn't prefer the front way?"

"No, I'd like very much to go by the wood path."

"Come along then."

They went out by the back door, which Carrington locked behind them, into the blackness of a cloudy night. "Rough going along here," said Carrington, "but it's not far. Shall we assume the prowler for convenience while I explain things?"

"Do."

"If he cut down from the wood path above the house, I mean to the north of the house on the way from Emeline Wakefield's, he wouldn't see the light in the library. The kitchen wing cuts it off."

"I understand."

"And my reading light wouldn't cast a glow outside. Very much the same thing that seems to have happened when he visited the Inn. Both places entirely dark, so far as he knew, downstairs. I'm giving you what evidence there is for a prowler, you understand?"

"Of course."

"Same thing at Edgewood."

"But at the Rigby Library—"

"I know, that does seem to break the chain. But if he'd been hanging about in the neighborhood at all he may very well have known that it is a library, and that anyone working late there would be alone. He'd make sure first. Look in. But he saw that he'd put Miss Bluett on the alert. Didn't chance it. For all he knew her desk might have been facing the other way. This afternoon he got her— from the rear."

"Quite possibly that's the way it was."

"One can't hope to follow the mental processes of such a being."

"No."

"Look out for your head, these pine branches hang down."

Pine needles underfoot now, pine branches overhead. The little circles of light from their torches got them through, and up a bank slippery with old leaves. Opposite them the woods hung dark, tree trunks looming.

"We're on the trail now," said Carrington. "Screened on both sides, no break through until we're behind the Inn."

"Pleasant walk in summer."

"And in winter; well protected from snow and wind."

They went silently, until Carrington stopped. "Here's the break through to Emeline's orchard. Nice apples. We have some of our own. You can see the Inn lights."

"I see them."

"Almost anywhere along behind the Inn you can get through to the grounds without trouble."

They went on. "Careful," said Carrington, "roots here. The trail is going back to jungle. You see now that the prowler must have had a torch."

"Absolutely."

"But with a torch there was no trick to it."

"None."

"Here's the break to the Library."

They left the path and made their way between old

sprawling shrubbery and trees, crossed the wall where Gamadge had sat that afternoon, and arrived at the head of the cellar steps. Carrington took out Hawkins' key.

"If you're not familiar with the library cellar," said Gamadge, "perhaps I might go first. I made the trip twice this afternoon. Place is rather cluttered."

"Go ahead."

He unlocked the door, and Gamadge went in. "Lock up behind you?" he suggested.

"Good idea." Carrington did so. They stood in the clean damp place, Gamadge's torch pointing to the wood-pile.

"Logs down," he said, and promptly stumbled. "Look out, all over the floor."

They picked their way across to the stairs. Carrington said: "Can you imagine negotiating these with a candle, and probably a bag or bottles under your other arm? Why weren't all our ancestors' servants crippled for life? Where *is* the light switch?"

"Up above, I suppose. Wait a minute." Gamadge went up, opened a door, hunted about. "Yes, all right."

The light went on. Carrington joined him in the back hall. They looked into the kitchen and the bathroom, and Gamadge turned another switch that lighted the back stairs.

"Going up there?" asked Carrington.

"Later."

"If I hadn't come you'd be doing all this alone? Gad, I envy you your nerves."

"I'm a bundle of nerves at all times."

"What absurdity."

Gamadge went along and turned the switch that lighted the book room. Carrington glanced down at the toppled books on the floor to the right, and looked at Gamadge.

"Yes, she was down there. They've cleaned up."

"Thank heaven."

"She sat at the desk working. I believe she was kneeling down looking at the books when her caller came on Thursday night. She must have been terribly frightened, but she wouldn't admit it. Well, the place is shut up tight enough now; hot as hell."

"What are you going to look for here, Gamadge?"

"I'm going to cast my eye over these criminology shelves." Gamadge moved to the left. Carrington laid his rifle on Miss Bluett's desk. He bent to the piles of books on the floor.

"Here's where this fellow belongs." He knelt on one knee, straightening the *Birds of Our Woodlands*. "Damn shame, how they've been kicked around. I'll stack 'em."

He picked up the thin volumes one by one, replaced loose pages, glanced at colored plates. His back was to Gamadge, who pulled volumes from the shelf in front of him and replaced them. Suddenly, as Carrington drew a page out of a book, he felt his wrist grasped. The sheet was pulled from his fingers. He twisted to look up. "What the—"

Gamadge had the page and was reading it. Carrington gasped: "What's that? What—"

"If you didn't know, why did you come here to look for it?"

"Are you—are you crazy?"

"Just the size of those bird book pages; but it's a sheet of your father's letter paper. The color's pretty nearly right, too, off-white. The old pages are yellowed. I mentioned the similarity of size and color and texture when I was in that bedroom this evening." Gamadge's voice was toneless. "I wouldn't blame anyone for making a mistake."

"Mistake?" Carrington snatched at the sheet in Gamadge's hand. Still on one knee and twisted back, he was ashen.

"Didn't you make one? Didn't you mistake a loose page from a bird book for this letter, and pull out the page, and find out your mistake after you killed him? That book on his night table was the wrong one, wasn't it? He must have changed them after you left him in the afternoon."

169

Carrington said in a whisper: "I don't know what you're talking about. What is that in your hand?"

"You wretched blundering fool, don't you know yet that if you're here it's on my invitation?"

Carrington stared at him, his face drawn into a mask.

"I had a theory," said Gamadge, "and I had to test it. And you carried out the test for me."

Carrington's head jerked sharply to the left; his hand went to his pocket; he whispered: "For God's sake, Gamadge, stand away from me."

Gamadge did so. Carrington's pistol exploded as the sheriff and White, the captain of state police, surged into the room from the passage. Ridley shouted: "Damn it, Gamadge, I knew you couldn't handle it." But Gamadge thought he had handled it pretty well.

White was on one knee beside the fallen body. Ridley watched him; when he turned to Gamadge he spoke not unamiably:

"Well, you couldn't know he had a gun in his pocket as well as that Winchester he brought."

"No."

"You fixed the act all right, and you had the sense to kick that log of wood when I made that noise in the cellar. Close quarters behind the furnace, I knocked something with my knee." He added, looking down at Carrington's body, "I couldn't believe you when you telephoned from Edgewood before supper. Neither could White when I told him. But our motto is, try anything."

Captain White got to his feet. He grunted: "Didn't think you'd get him here if he was guilty."

"He had to come," said Gamadge. "He hadn't had a chance before, and he had to take this one. I'd remarked that this paper is very much like the pages in the bird books. If he let me come here alone, what mightn't I have poked around and discovered?"

"He had this afternoon," objected White, scowling at the paper in Gamadge's hand. "Why not get the thing then, whatever it is?"

"This afternoon he had barely time to arrange the

170

evidence upstairs after the murder. How did he know Willie Stapler wouldn't raise an alarm sooner?"

"Miss Bluett might have found that thing"—the sheriff jerked his head at what Gamadge was holding—"any time."

"She had Thursday evening to find it, and Carrington didn't know it was here until after he'd killed his father that night. Then the Library was full of you people, and afterwards locked. He knew she hadn't found it, and he thought he had days, while she was away, to invent some reasonable excuse to get in alone. He never dreamed she'd be here this afternoon. When he found she was, did he waste time? But he couldn't search eleven books for this."

"What in time is it?"

"It's the beginning of his father's proposal of marriage to Rose Jenner."

18. LOVE LETTER

Labor Day was bright and mild; Mrs. Gamadge and young Henry came up to Westbury by train, were met by Gamadge, and had lunch at Edgewood. Afterwards Mrs. Gamadge, Mrs. Turnbull, Miss Studley, Miss Pepper, Mrs. Norbury and Mr. Haynes sat in the lounge while young Henry staggered from one to the other, the Monster in his arms, calling it Nice Kitty.

Mr. Haynes did not seem the worse for his shocking experience with the law; in fact he was very talkative and cheerful, and Gamadge remarked to Clara that now Haynes had seen life in the raw and could retire on the anecdote. "Dine out on it for years."

"Poor Mrs. Turnbull. I'm afraid somebody will marry her for her money."

"Are you? Perhaps you're right."

Gamadge left the party and walked down to the Wakefield Inn. Miss Wakefield would not be there—she was with Lydia Carrington; but Yates had telephoned that Rose Jenner and he would like to see Gamadge if he could spare the time, and were in Miss Wakefield's office. "We won't be interrupted, Homans has got a Descendant to fix her hair."

"Fix—oh yes. Has she?"

"Descendant of a Chapley lady's maid; does all the hair in Frazer's Mills from a great-great-aunt's recipe."

"I'd like to see the result." Gamadge added: "You sound very brisk and happy."

"I am."

"Good. Be with you."

Walking down the street to the Inn, Gamadge marveled at the transformation in The Mills, wrought overnight. People did not, it is true, look gay, some of them were downcast; but there were people, lots of people; on the footways, on the porches, everywhere. Doors stood wide, old inhabitants sunned themselves in the yards. It was a different place.

Yates and Rose Jenner were in the office, waiting for him. He took her hand.

"Nice try of yours last night, Miss Jenner; I knew you were fighting for him."

"I'd do anything—anything—for the Carringtons."

"You felt that you were doing what your guardian would have wanted?"

"What Lydia wanted. What my stepmother would have wanted. She was a Carrington. I'd never heard of them until she married my father; there's nothing she didn't try to do for me. Mr. Gamadge, you don't know what she was like; and we were happy together. When she died I lost everything—or thought I had. And then my guardian sent and saved me again. And Lydia was so kind. I was just a bother and a nuisance, but they were so kind. Even Lawrence—until . . ."

"Until he fell in love with you?"

She stood looking at him silently, as if unable to speak. He went on gently:

"I was sure that Lawrence Carrington had committed the murders; but I was sure he wouldn't commit murder for motives of gain, and in cold blood. There must have been some other reason, the kind of thing, suddenly discovered, that drives a man like Carrington temporarily mad."

She nodded sombrely.

"He had accumulated rage ever since his father sank the family fortunes in an annuity; I could understand that. He had ceased to think of George Carrington as a father at all. Perhaps he had discovered that he was going to lose this place, which he loved."

"Yes, he loved it."

"Motive, but not enough. What had lighted that sudden fire in Lawrence Carrington's brain, and impelled that civilized, inhibited man to commit such a crime? Well, some intense form of jealousy might do it—has done it before. Was it a crime of passion? Frustrated passion? I wondered." He looked at Rose Jenner and smiled faintly.

"He loved me; I couldn't marry him. Mr. Gamadge, he was out of his senses when he killed my guardian."

"But he killed Miss Bluett to save himself from discovery."

"Can't people go mad from fear?"

"They can. Call it madness. You did your best for him; and his sister had a try at helping him, too, didn't she?"

"I realized then that *she* knew."

"Knew because he didn't care whether doors were locked or not?"

"We knew the way he felt about his father. He couldn't hide it. He hated him—on account of the annuity first. Mr. Gamadge, you frightened me yesterday at the Library, when you said that about the newspapers; you didn't believe in the maniac. I was so frightened on Lawrence's account that I got that stick of wood, just before dinner, and hid it in the trellis. I had to do something."

"You succeeded in knocking him almost silly."

"I didn't realize that Lawrence would know then I suspected him."

"And at supper Miss Carrington put on *her* show, and he knew she suspected him."

Rose put her hand in her coat pocket, brought out a square gray envelope, and offered it to Gamadge. "I want you to read this."

"Now," said Yates, "you'll know what she's really made of, Gamadge."

Gamadge looked at it. It was addressed *Rose,* and on the flap was an engraved *Lawrence Carrington* in block letters. "He left this for you?"

"Lydia found it in his desk. It wasn't hidden; he was so sure there would never be any need for it. I don't want to see it again. If it weren't for Lydia I'd ask you to burn it, but somebody might blame her in some way, and he wrote it to prevent that."

Gamadge turned the envelope in his hand. "But you don't want it?"

"It's a frightful letter."

Yates said: "It was written to distress her, but she won't destroy it. I've read it, Gamadge; when you've read it you'll understand these ghastly murders better."

Rose turned her face away. "I never dreamed that my guardian wanted to marry me. He never said a word. And I wouldn't have married him; but Lawrence thought I would."

Gamadge asked: "It never occurred to you that your guardian had reasons of self-interest in keeping you away from young company and banishing your friends?"

"No, it never did."

"But you had a feeling that he wouldn't care even for Yates?"

"I only thought he was a little unfair."

"I'm glad you had spirit enough to see young Mr. Yates away from home."

Yates observed: "Selfish old brute."

"Yes, he was selfish," said Rose. "I know he was. But when I had nobody, he saved me."

"I'm glad your loyalty has limits. You'd have done anything for the Carringtons—but marry them." Gamadge looked at the letter in his hand. "But you're loyal enough. Thank you for trusting me with this, Miss Jenner; if it isn't needed—and I don't know why it should be—I'll return it to you for burning."

"Mr. Gamadge—" she hesitated. "You'll see when you read it that he meant to kill himself if anything went wrong for him. And he had his gun last night. Did you let him do it?"

"That's putting myself into your hands; but I'm glad to show my admiration by doing so. I knew he must have a gun—I knew that rifle was camouflage. If he hadn't known *I* had one—but never mind that. At the end

175

he begged me, almost in words, to let him use his. Thinking of you and Miss Carrington, I did let him use it." He added: "I'd have been still more willing to let him use it if I'd known that you were capable of saving a letter such as this one must be, saving it instead of burning it, running the risk of having it published, for a Carrington's sake."

She put her hand into his again, and then turned away. "I must get back to the house. Don't come, Garry. You want to talk to Mr. Gamadge."

Yates went to the front door with her; while he was gone, Gamadge opened and read the letter. It was dated: *Two o'clock, Friday Morning, 27th August,* and it began abruptly:

Rosie, you know I loved you; you can imagine whether I love you now. But why do I write as if you were ever going to see this? There is no chance whatever, so far as I can judge, that you will see it; but who can tell? So I leave it—for Lydia's protection and your enlightenment. I shouldn't care to depart this life without letting you know that I had discovered your game here, and had ruined it. Now, whatever happens, you won't be the mistress of this house and of all our valued things; and you won't turn Lydia and me out of our home: all that my father left us of our patrimony.

I suppose you would have persuaded him to sell the place—you wouldn't be satisfied with a widow's share, would you?

As I imply above, I shall remove myself abruptly from the scene if anything goes wrong; I shall not stay for protestations or the long farce of self-defense. And I will admit that one mistake was made by me, though it won't be fatal. I shall rectify it. Nobody will look through those bird books now—Miss Bluett won't be in the Library for days.

176

What happened was absurd. This afternoon—it seems a long time ago—I wandered to the south doorway of my father's room and looked in. He was writing, using one of the bird books for a writing-block. When I came in he closed the book—hastily, I thought— and laid it on his bed table. Then his tray came, and I had an opportunity—hidden by the bed curtain—of glancing at what he was anxious I shouldn't see.

One glance was quite enough to show me that Lydia and I were going to acquire a stepmother, and suffer final disinheritance. But it showed me more. When you refused me, dear Rosie, I humbly admitted that I was not only unworthy of you but too old for you. But your guardian wasn't too old for you, was he? You were out for bigger game than Lawrence Carrington and his five thousand a year. He'd have taken out life insurance for you, wouldn't he, though he never did for us? How demure you have been, and what fools Lydia and I were not to know why that old man was keeping you to himself!

Well, I love my sister Lydia, and I love my own comfort too. And I loved you once. If I did go mad there in that bedroom, when I read those lines and realized all they meant, I didn't show it. I'm used to repressing my feelings, you know. Did Lydia or my father ever guess how I once felt about you? So I left the letter where it was, a half inch showing beyond the page, and I retired. How was I to know that he'd take up another of the bird books from the chair beside the bed, and lay the one with the letter in it in the other's place on top of the pile? How was he to know that Hattie Bluett would send for the set, and that poor Lydia would creep in and take them—all but one—while he was asleep?

The wrong book lay where the other had lain, on the night table, *with a page protruding*. A loose page.

And when I arrived after my night walk, a little before eleven, I put out my hand in the darkness—that was after my father was dead, you know—and pulled out what I thought was the letter. I couldn't delay, never looked at it.

I soon discovered my mistake, and I had to return and replace the loose page; I leave no clues, you know! You wouldn't believe the trouble I've taken over details.

The proposal of marriage was in the Rigby Library; but I had looked in on Hattie Bluett while I was in the process of building up the Prowler identity, and she can't have touched *Woodland Birds*. She was still working on big sets of bound magazines. Now she won't be in the library again, as I said, for many a day. I'll make an excuse to get there—happy thought, the forgotten book!—and all will be well.

So here I sit with my glass of brandy beside me, cheerfully enough, writing you this letter that you will never read. I almost wish that you could read it. I wish you knew what Lydia's and my lives have been —how we were crushed and discouraged and devoured, taken for granted and at last disinherited. He let Nadine die, he ruined Lydia's life, because they wouldn't completely efface themselves; he can't ruin what's left of mine.

This is melodrama; I'd better stop. I've had a good deal of brandy. Will you think better of me as a husband now, Rose? If you do, what fun it will be to turn you down.

As Gamadge finished reading, Yates came back. "Well?" Yates asked it with raised eyebrows. "Call it madness?"

"A weak man pursued by furies. They overtook him."

"You didn't know all that, but you guessed it was Carrington."

"I didn't know anything, but I guessed it was Carrington almost from the first. I built up a theory, and last night I tested it—that's all."

"All? I'd like to hear the build-up."

"Glad to oblige."

"You owe me something, you know." Yates regarded him with a half-smile. "Going to the police behind my back after I telephoned you on Friday."

"How else could I have got into the Carrington house without giving you away?"

"Couldn't you have mentioned the fact to me?"

"Well, no. Not after you told me that you were calling me on behalf of Miss Rose Jenner."

"I see. Needed a free hand, did you?"

"If I had found reason to suspect Miss Jenner, I couldn't very well have taken you into my confidence, could I? You called me in; but not, I assumed, as special pleader or counsel for anybody's defense. I couldn't be that, knowing nothing of the case and nothing of Miss Jenner beyond the fact that she had no alibi."

"Knowing her, I knew she'd be all right with you. But I hadn't realized how the chips fly when you hew to the line. You had me a little nervous. Well, we know the outcome; tell me how you arrived at it."

"Glad to oblige."

They sat on opposite sides of Miss Wakefield's desk. Gamadge picked up a bronze paperweight in the form of a pacing horse.

"That," said Yates, "is Bay Bayard. The animals with proper names were Wakefield animals."

"And Lydia and Lawrence Carrington had to know their stud catechism, though they weren't interested."

"And neither of them had the courage to break away."

19. NIGHT WALK

"I arrived at it," said Gamadge, "by way of the maniac
theory. The idea was that there must have been a maniac
because there was no motive for the murders, no link
between the near-victims and the actual victim, and an
infinite capacity on the part of the murderer for taking
risks.

"You and the sheriff and I-don't-know-how-many-other
people insisted on those points to me; and the points were
valid. But if the maniac took risks—wilder risks than such
maniacs as our old friend the Düsseldorf Monster took, for
instance—he seemed to have an infinite capacity for getting
away with them. It looked as though he *was* an inhabitant
of Frazer's Mills, as the sheriff suspected; and it looked
to me as if he might not be quite so crazy as all that after
all.

"But if he wasn't crazy, there must have been a motive."

"That was the trouble," said Yates eagerly. "There was
no motive."

"There must have been one, and therefore I could
make some eliminations. Anybody who was in Frazer's
Mills by accident that night, or on legitimate other business, could be eliminated. You were out, from my point
of view, because you hadn't intended to be here on Thursday night at all; they could prove that in Westbury."

"Well, thanks," said Yates, laughing.

Gamadge cast a severe glance at him. "This is a problem, my good fellow; not a feast of friendship."

"I see."

180

"Miss Wakefield was out because you, already out, alibied her. Don't talk to me about local reputation. . . ."

"I won't."

"Carrington had one—that of a highly respectable man of cultivated tastes, devoted to his charming father. Miss Homans and the Silvers senior alibied one another. The Silver boy remained a possibility. Miss Bluett? No, she went home with Willie Stapler before Carrington was killed.

"The people at Edgewood? Miss Pepper and Mrs. Norbury out—they were together after ten thirty. Miss Studley out—she answered Miss Wakefield's telephone call before she could have returned to Edgewood from the Carringtons'. Haynes out—he had been sent here for definite reasons by his doctor. Mrs. Turnbull ditto. For either of them to arrive at a strange place and find a mortal enemy there—no; logic doesn't have to deal with such coincidences."

"You don't mention Motley, but he was out too—sent up here by his doctor."

"Motley? Oh, yes. Motley was out. The natives were eliminated by the police, *pace* Vines. I was left with young Silver, the Carringtons and Rose Jenner. Why should the Carringtons or Rose Jenner eliminate the man who kept them all in luxury? And why should they try to eliminate Mrs. Norbury, Miss Bluett, and old Mr. Compson?

"Struggling for a link, I found none to connect those three as murder victims; but I found a link between the Carrington house and Edgewood, the Library and the Wakefield Inn.

"Anybody from the Carrington house might well visit Edgewood to consult Miss Studley about George Carrington's thermo-therapy; any of them might conceivably mistake old Mrs. Norbury's room for Miss Studley's office, which is just above it and may be entered freely night or day. Anybody from the Carrington house might stop in at the Library to have a word with Miss Bluett about the Carrington donation. Anybody from the Carrington house might call on old Mr. Compson, say to arrange for a game of chess. Would young Silver have any such excuse for a visit to those people?

"And who from the Carrington house could excusably visit *all* of them at half past ten of a rainy night?"

Yates said after a moment: "The women wouldn't drop in on Compson."

"They wouldn't indeed. Who but Lawrence Carrington could make those visits and explain himself if caught?"

Yates said: "I don't know how he could explain himself."

"Let's analyze the risk he ran; but first let's look at the man who ran the risk. He's in his raincoat, he's the son of a local magnate, he's known to all. He's the town's intellectual, no doubt looked upon as dreamy. His goings and comings are part of the native scene. He, if anyone, would be forgiven for absent-mindedness.

"He arrives at Edgewood; the place is in darkness below stairs, and the side door is unlocked. The second floor corridor is in darkness too. He walks in and fumbles at Mrs. Norbury's door—he'd have known which it was from previous reconnaissance. Who's to catch him? Even if Mrs. Norbury makes a noise he'll be out of the place in a few seconds, through the shrubbery and on the wood path in a minute more. But what if he is caught? He can say that he forgot which floor Miss Studley's office was on. He can apologize in embarrassment and back away.

"At the Library, if Miss Bluett pursues him, she'll find Lawrence Carrington fumbling with dropped keys, or a pipe lost in the bushes. He'll explain that he dropped his keys or his pipe while trying her latch."

"And at the Inn," said Yates, "he couldn't resist scaring the living daylights out of old Compson with that fire axe. He scared the living daylights out of me."

"But after he'd put the fire axe on the floor and knocked at Mr. Compson's door, how long do you suppose it took him to get out of the Inn by the side entrance, and get home? I've seen that layout. Seconds to do the job, home in five minutes—less. Once at home he could answer the telephone; once at home"—Gamadge leaned forward, his arms on the desk—"if there were any premature disturbance on account of his activities, he could call the whole thing off.

"For he had planned that campaign with the knowledge that there was no serious risk of any kind for him until the murder had been committed. Until the very moment of the murder he could drop the whole thing. At any moment of that night walk, at Edgewood, or the Library, or the Inn, if he were caught he could abandon his project forever. The prowler would be a local mystery, never cleared up and with no consequences.

"At none of those places—until he arrived at the Inn— had he done anything to cause great excitement; people don't start a panic at night or call the police in for nothing."

"But at the Inn it was only chance that kept Miss Wakefield from telephoning Carrington first."

"Chance. You both acted normally. And if she'd telephoned Carrington, he'd have answered. People talk these scares over, as I said, before they take action. As a matter of fact Carrington had time after the murder to leave his house again—the maniac's trail—and come in again by the back door."

Gamadge sat back and felt for his cigarettes. He lighted one and looked at it. "I was getting on," he said complacently. "I had a possible suspect with a possible motive—some state of mind connected with Miss Rose Jenner—and I had decided that the night walk was a plant."

Yates said: "Well, that was lovely. Do you always work on pure assumption?"

Gamadge looked at him with mild surprise. "I thought you'd remember that I also had a fact."

"That's good. What was it?"

"You ought to know; you were the first person to mention it to me—up by the pond. Then the sheriff mentioned it, and then Miss Bluett did, and finally Lawrence Carrington was good enough to tell me all about it last night."

"Hanged if I remember what it was."

"It was that touch of the unusual that one always looks for and hopes to find in the background of a crime. Something unexpected, something off schedule, something that might possibly have had unusual results. It wasn't much —just the fact that Miss Bluett had sent for a last consignment of books from the Carringtons, had sent for them only a few hours before George Carrington was murdered, and had got them days ahead of time. Miss Carrington had collected them and sent them off hastily, and Lawrence Carrington might not have known that they were gone.

"Nothing to think of until Miss Bluett was murdered. After she was murdered—wouldn't you have thought about them in my place?

"For since I wasn't looking for a maniac, Miss Bluett's death meant only one thing to me—she had been killed because she was a danger to somebody. Why a danger? As a blackmailer? She didn't strike me as the stuff of which blackmailers are made, and from what others told me about her I couldn't imagine her as a blackmailer. Miss Bluett was quite singleminded. Nor would such a type, if she had recognized the prowler on Thursday night, have kept the knowledge to herself; duty and self-importance would forbid.

"How much more probable that she was a danger because she was a librarian. As a librarian she was the only person ever likely to examine those books, which might have left the Carrington house without the knowledge of Lawrence Carrington. He couldn't have known about them when he visited the Library on the night walk, or I suppose he'd have committed the Bluett murder then. And he can't have known that she was going back to the Library to work yesterday afternoon; when he found that out, after he left me at Edgewood, he knew that he mustn't risk letting her make a discovery. After her murder he couldn't wait to examine the bird books—he had no time.

"He would return as soon as he safely could, not too soon for safety. I supplied him with an excuse to return, and a strong reason to return with me; I had remarked that his father's letter paper resembled the pages of the bird book in texture and size, and he was afraid that I might make discoveries myself. I wondered at the time whether some mistake of the kind had been made, whether the death of Miss Bluett wasn't connected with some confusion—in the hurry and excitement of the Carrington murder—between a page of the bird book and a sheet of that writing paper, with writing on it.

"I could only make my test; and as you know, the test didn't fail."

"You'd already called the sheriff and arranged for an ambush."

"I called him as soon as I knew he'd be at the Tavern, after I'd had a chance to think the Bluett murder over. He and White were only too glad to try the thing out—*they're* not sentimental about Frazer's Mills. So they waited in the cellar—they were afraid Carrington might have a look round upstairs—and came up after us. I had that idea that Carrington might still have business at the Rigby Library; I didn't know at all what he was going to do. I could only watch him and see."

"He never knew you'd watch him?"

"I had to keep him reassured about that before we went. It wasn't too easy. It's never a pleasant thing, you know, to play the part of agent provocateur—I had to keep my mind on Miss Harriet Bluett, a nice woman, who never got her bus ride."

"How did you keep him happy?" asked Yates. "In your place I don't think I'd have had compunctions."

"Oh, he had his points; for instance, much as he hated Rose Jenner by that time, he didn't allow me to fix guilt on her."

"Were you pretending to do that?" Yates raised his eyebrows.

"Well, I had to convince him that I wasn't suspecting *him*. I was afraid that he'd do what he says in that letter he'd have done at the first alarm—remove himself from the scene. I had to get him to the Library and find out what he was after there. You know"—Gamadge looked innocently at Yates—"I'd pretty well worked out her position in the affair."

"Had you really."

"Well, if she supplied a motive for the crime—that thwarted love motive—she couldn't have been in it with Lawrence Carrington. I decided that her anxiety on his account must be altruism."

"That was nice of you."

"And I was a good deal cleverer than Carrington had been about that proposal of marriage. Those few opening lines that George Carrington had written were no more than a flat request for her hand. If Lawrence Carrington hadn't been blind with accumulated rage he ought to have realized that a proposal of marriage isn't written—to somebody living under the same roof—if the answer is certain to be favorable. In that case a written proposal is bound to be a brief—an argument; George Carrington wasn't sure of Rose Jenner. His previous attitude to her became clear, and she emerged to me as a generous character struggling in the toils of her own gratitude."

Yates burst out laughing. "I'd told you so."

"You were in love, my boy."

"That disqualified me, did it?"

"Certainly. I'm the only man I know of who ever judged his future wife correctly; but even I didn't expect others to share my judgment."

They looked at each other, grinning amiably. Yates said: "Well, anyhow, we know pretty well what Lawrence Carrington did on Thursday night. He'd had a look at that proposal of marriage, and he had a brainstorm. He decided the marriage mustn't take place."

"And he decided that his father—whom he hadn't regarded as a father for a long time—must die before seeing Rose Jenner again. Nobody must ever know about the letter, which constituted a motive for murder."

"Rose was rushing off, presumably to the movies, wouldn't be back until about half past eleven. And the front of the house would be in darkness—Miss Carrington wouldn't be near the parlor bedroom.

"She wouldn't disturb the invalid until he called. Well, the campaign was planned; the whole idea being to build up the picture of a homicidal maniac. He knew every inch of the way, he knew the town and the people in it. He didn't need properties; all he had to do was to pull on a pair of woollen socks over his shoes before he got home."

Yates sat for a minute thinking it over; then he shook himself free of the bad dream. "I hate The Mills now," he said. "I can't wait to get Rose away."

"Clara's sold on it. We're booking rooms here. But I must say," observed Gamadge wistfully, "that I'd like to have known the place in its vintage years; tasted the full flavor and bouquet."

The triple blast of a motor horn came to them from somewhere, a blast so peremptory that they got up with one accord and went through the hall to the front porch. A tremendous closed car was slowly coming to a stop at the curb below the Inn; it looked as though it had been carved out of a solid block of onyx, and inlaid with platinum.

A uniformed chauffeur got down and opened the car door. He helped an old gentleman to alight; an old gentleman wrapped in fleecy camel's hair, and wearing a cap which matched the shepherd's plaid of his trousers. Between cap and collar appeared a face crimsoned by good whiskey and golf in the sun; it was adorned by a cropped and snowy moustache.

Along the street and from across the way people surged up to the car; Mrs. Stapler, Willie Stapler, and Mrs. Broadbent; a gaffer on two sticks; Miss Studley from the north and Officer Adey from the south. The old gentleman stopped on his way across the sidewalk, one arm supported by the chauffeur, the other raised in benevolent salute to the peasantry.

Miss Studley rushed up and took his free arm.

Gamadge said: "The durbar."

187

"What?" asked Yates.

"Last of the vintage crop."

Three young men, certainly newsmen, dashed from the Tavern. The old gentleman was now proceeding up the walk to the Inn, and the newsmen got in front of him and walked backward as he advanced. He conversed with them in a hoarse and resonant voice:

"Compson, my name is Compson. Yes, that is my house opposite the Carringtons'—it is now a ladies' seminary. Can't run a house nowadays. Why am I here? Delighted to inform you: I am here to attend the funeral of my old friend George Carrington, and his son's funeral, and also the funeral of Harriet Bluett. And I am here to offer my services, for what they are worth, to Miss Lydia Carrington. She will need support and comfort.

"By all means print what I say. It is all I have to say; and so, gentlemen, if you will be so good as to get to the devil out from under my feet . . ."

But the cortège had arrived at the foot of the porch steps, and the newsmen gleefully introduced Yates.

Mr. Compson stood still, looking up at the young man. He said, "Emeline Wakefield's transient, who has my room."

"I moved out this morning, Mr. Compson. I didn't hurt anything."

"I daresay not. You are not to blame, Mr. Yates, for Emeline's cheeseparing. And if I see *that* remark in print" —he glanced ferociously to right and left—"I shall instruct my lawyer to sue in behalf of Emeline Wakefield, and I shall pay his bill."

The reporters, highly gratified by this scoop on local color, hurried back to the Tavern and the telephone. Mr. Compson, with the assistance of his two helpers, slowly mounted the steps. Once safely on the porch, he stopped to look at Yates with fiery blue eyes.

"Very unfortunate that I wasn't here on Thursday night," he said. "If I had been, there would have been no murders."

"No, sir?"

"No. I would have caught him."

Miss Studley was a Descendant, with vestigial traces of feudalism; but she had done something to the wheel of destiny. Bravely, therefore, if faintly, she put in a word for her oddest inmate:

"This is Mr. Gamadge, Mr. Compson. Mr. Gamadge did catch him."

Mr. Compson turned his head with deliberation, looked Gamadge slowly up and down, acknowledged his existence as a member of the human race with a slight nod, and remarked: "Yes. So I understand. Too late."

"No," said Gamadge, "not too late."

"You mean for vengeance? Let me tell you, sir, that George Carrington—yes, and Hattie Bluett—would rest quieter in their graves if the newspapers could have stuck to the prowler."

The trio disappeared into the house. Gamadge and Yates exchanged a glance of awe.

"Do you get the flavor now?" asked Yates.

"All of it; and the bouquet."

A Savage Place

By Robert B. Parker

Called away from his Boston turf, crack detective Spenser takes on the assignment of protecting Candy Sloan, a glamorous Hollywood television reporter on the verge of breaking the biggest story of her career. The glittering storybook world of Hollywood is laid bare as Candy and Spenser seek to prove allegations of mob payoffs into the movie business.

"Robert B. Parker continues to write tough private eye stories with exceptional wit, compassion and intelligence."
$2.95   —The Houston Post

Classic Tales by
the Mistress of Mystery

AGATHA
CHRISTIE

☐ An Overdose of Death.................$2.50   16780-9
☐ The Big Four.............................$2.25   10562-5
☐ Elephants Can Remember..........$2.50   12329-1
☐ The Labors of Hercules $2.50   14620-8
☐ Partners in Crime......................$2.50   16848-1
☐ They Came to Baghdad..............$1.95   18700-1
☐ 13 for Luck...............................$1.95   18753-2
☐ Three Blind Mice
   and Other Stories.....................$2.50   15867-2
☐ Why Didn't They Ask Evans $2.50   10704-0
☐ Witness for the Prosecution $2.50   19619-1